"Come on, Dare, move your butt," Casey said, tugging on his arm.

"Yes, ma'am." He let go of the edge of the pool—and sank. Casey grabbed him, supporting him, her arms wrapped around his chest. His groping hands caught the edge of the pool and he pulled himself toward it, trapping her body between his and the cement.

Casey felt herself begin to ache deep inside with the need to love him once more. Could he feel her pulse throbbing? Could he hear her heart pounding? Did he know how much she wanted him?

His hot, hungry eyes gave her the answer.

"Look, Dare, maybe we better postpone this until tomorrow," she whispered, so breathless she could barely speak. "You're already exhausted."

"Stop treating me like a child."

Lowering his head, he seared a kiss across her lips, shocking her, stealing the air out of her lungs. Dare had never kissed her this way before. His kisses had always been gentle, considerate . . . never raw, never hot, never demanding.

For the first time in her life, Dare was kissing her as if she were a woman. . . .

WHAT ARE *LOVESWEPT* ROMANCES?

They are stories of true romance and touching emotion. We believe those two very important ingredients are constants in our highly sensual and very believable stories in the LOVESWEPT *line. Our goal is to give you, the reader, stories of consistently high quality that may sometimes make you laugh, sometimes make you cry, but are always fresh and creative and contain many delightful surprises within their pages.*

Most romance fans read an enormous number of books. Those they truly love, they keep. Others may be traded with friends and soon forgotten. We hope that each LOVESWEPT *romance will be a treasure—a "keeper." We will always try to publish*

LOVE STORIES YOU'LL NEVER FORGET
BY AUTHORS YOU'LL ALWAYS REMEMBER

The Editors

Loveswept® 720

DAREDEVIL

LYNNE
BRYANT

BANTAM BOOKS
NEW YORK · TORONTO · LONDON · SYDNEY · AUCKLAND

DAREDEVIL
A Bantam Book / December 1994

ISBN 0-553-44394-1

Published simultaneously in the United States and Canada

Bantam Books are published by Bantam Books, a division of Bantam Doubleday Dell Publishing Group, Inc. Its trademark, consisting of the words "Bantam Books" and the portrayal of a rooster, is Registered in U.S. Patent and Trademark Office and in other countries. Marca Registrada. Bantam Books, 1540 Broadway, New York, New York 10036.

PRINTED IN THE UNITED STATES OF AMERICA

OPM 0 9 8 7 6 5 4 3 2 1

To the Greater Vancouver Chapter of
RWA.
Thanks for all your help.

With special thanks to the gals in
"R Group":
Mary, Mavis, Molly, Valda, and Pat.
It is a joy working with you.

And especially to Mom and Dad,
two very special people
who know all about pain
and about love

PROLOGUE

Knuckles pressed against her lips, Casey Boone gazed down at the giant of a man who lay so deathly pale—so deathly still—on the hospital bed. Darrick King. Her larger-than-life hero who had tossed her into the air when she'd been a child. The tough-but-tender Texan who had taught her the meaning of love.

The man she had told to stay out of her life.

"I'm sorry, Casey, my dear, but there's a very good chance he won't walk again," Dr. Bell said, awkwardly patting her shoulder, trying to avoid the tumble of red curls that cascaded around it.

"It can't be true," she whispered, her voice husky with suppressed tears. Dr. Bell was the chief of staff of the Lone Star Children's Hospital where Casey worked, and was, in her eyes, the best neurosurgeon in Texas. But this was Dare he was talking about.

2

Three days earlier Dare had been injured when rebels had attacked his team of firefighters while they'd been battling a raging oil-well fire in the mountains of Colombia. Injured so badly, he was lying immobile, unconscious, his six-foot-six muscular frame filling every available inch of the hospital bed. A cast covered his body from rib cage to midthigh; an IV ran into his left arm, which was restrained to the bed rail; a white bandage was wrapped around his broad shoulder; and the rest of his tanned, rock-hard body was covered with abrasions and bruises.

"You never can tell with spinal injuries, but I think you should be prepared for the worst," Dr. Bell said, looking up at Casey, his blue eyes, behind the thick lenses of his wire-rimmed glasses, kind and full of concern. "Amazingly enough, King's spinal column wasn't fractured," he continued, "but the nerves and muscles in his lower back and legs took a real beating. We won't know the extent of the damage until the swelling goes down."

Casey leaned over the bed rail and picked up Dare's right hand, deliberately forcing Dr. Bell's words out of her mind. Her job as a physical therapist at the hospital meant daily contact with children who had spinal-cord injuries; she didn't want even to *think* about what the future might hold for Dare.

"I'm going to stay with him," she said, her voice still husky but filled with determination.

"He seems to rest a lot easier when you're holding his hand," Dr. Bell agreed tentatively as his gaze swept over her, taking in the purple smudges under her emerald-green eyes, the tension in her spine, the exhausted droop of her slim shoulders. "But are you sure you're up to it? You haven't moved from his side since you brought him in from the ranch."

That had been eighteen hours and twenty-three minutes ago, Casey noted, glancing at her watch. Eighteen hours and twenty-three minutes of holding Dare's hand while he'd been X-rayed and prodded and poked . . . and telling him stories because the sound of her voice also seemed to soothe him . . . and watching as spasm after spasm of pain racked his body. An eternity.

But it was nothing compared with the thirty-six hours of sheer terror she'd endured as she'd waited with the rest of the King family at the Regent Ranch for Duke and Dev to bring their brother home. She'd waited and prayed in the family chapel—and wondered, helplessly, hopelessly, if Dare, too, would desert her the way the other people she'd loved had deserted her.

Miraculously Dare had been alive when King Oil's jet had landed on the private strip at the ranch, and she had ridden with him to the hospital in the ambulance she'd had standing by.

"I'll stay with him," Casey repeated softly. "At least until he wakes up."

"That shouldn't be too long, my dear, now that

we've reduced his analgesic. Once he's conscious and rational, we'll remove the cast, but he'll be in a lot of pain, you know."

"Yes." She shuddered, sick to the bone with the thought of Dare suffering pain.

"And he'll need a lot of reassurance."

"I know." By the time Dare regained consciousness, she would be chock-full of reassurance, she told herself firmly. She sighed, then spared Dr. Bell a quick glance. "Would you please phone Madre and tell her that Dare is all right." Keeping the news of Dare's injury from the press had been the key factor when they'd made arrangements to put him into the private children's hospital, which was located halfway between Houston and the Regent Ranch. It was also the reason why his family wasn't haunting the halls. She knew how desperately worried everyone—especially his mother—must be.

"Better yet, I'll drive out to the ranch and see them," Dr. Bell said. "And don't worry. I'm not about to burden them with the bad news." After another look at the man on the bed and another pat on Casey's shoulder, he left the room.

Blinking back the tears, which had been burning for release ever since Madre had phoned her about Dare's accident, Casey continued to grip Dare's big hand with hers . . . remembering another time, long ago, when her hand was very small and his had held hers.

"Come on, princess, get up!" he'd told her,

smiling the special smile he reserved for her. "You can't learn to ride if you're sitting on the ground."

He dusted her off and placed his hand under her chin. "You ready to try again?"

She was only four, but her faith in Dare gave her courage, and she rode her horse that day. She also remembered the pride in his face when she'd won her first blue ribbon the following year. He'd been fourteen, but not the least bit self-conscious about rooting for his princess.

Funny, she never thought of her father or her invalid mother in those early memories. Just Dare. Always Dare.

"Don't worry, Dare, you'll walk," she said, leaning over to speak the words softly into his ear. "I'll help you."

It was the least she could do for the man who'd been at the center of her life for her first twenty-two years. First as her much-adored "big brother," then as her father's world-renowned partner, and finally, for a few short weeks, as her marvelous lover and soon-to-be husband.

Raising his hand, she pressed the back of it against her cheek and held it there, gazing down at him, her eyes swimming with tears. He had to get well. The *Daredevil* had to walk and run and ride the range again.

She turned her head slightly and nuzzled a kiss against his knuckles, then drew in a ragged breath, and another. Finally she lowered his hand and stared at it through a fresh film of tears. There were new scars on his knuckles, she noted suddenly. How had he gotten those scars? And why didn't she know about them?

Because she had forfeited the right to know when she'd told Dare to get out of her life.

She stroked the pads of her fingers in a soothing motion across the scars and along his thick, muscular fingers. She remembered, with a shiver of heart-stopping delight, just how tender those fingers could be, how they'd caressed her and teased her and taught her things about her body—intimate things she'd never known before.

Now they squeezed her hand in a bone-crushing vise as another spasm seized Dare's big body. With trembling fingers, she brushed the shaggy, sweat-soaked brown hair off his broad forehead and gazed at his rugged features, wishing he hadn't been hurt. Wishing he were pretending to be asleep. Wishing he would open his gingerbread eyes and smile at her.

It had been three years since she'd seen his lazy, sexy, heartwarming smile. Three long years, during which she'd kept reassuring herself that nothing would happen to Dare—now that she no longer loved him.

Refusing to love Dare hadn't kept him safe.

It was time to face facts. Dare was just like her father. He would keep on killing wild wells until they killed him.

She shivered, chilled to the bone with despair. With her free hand she picked up the shawl she'd been wearing in the chapel when the jet had arrived and draped it over her head.

On the bed, Dare moved restlessly and moaned softly. He was regaining consciousness, Casey realized. Oh, Lord, please let him stay under a little while longer. Don't make him face the pain and the uncertainty that waited for him. He wasn't strong enough for the ordeal yet.

And neither was she.

Inch by torturous inch Dare fought his way through the layers of pain that threatened to suck him down into a black hole so deep, he would never emerge. At first he'd been tempted to stop fighting, to give in to the pain, to let it carry him away to a place where he would never be lonely again. Then something had happened, and he knew he couldn't give in. Someone had taken his hand . . . someone he'd been waiting for . . . for such a long time.

Slowly he opened his eyes . . . and gave a soul-deep sigh of relief. His wait was over.

Casey was there.

She was standing beside him, a misty vision of loveliness. He smiled at her, feeling so doggone happy to see her that, for a weak moment, he was afraid he might cry. She smiled back, her wide, sunny smile that always made him feel so good inside. Her glorious red hair was covered with something white. He strained to focus. That's right. Casey was going to wear her grandmother's veil today. Their wedding day.

He swallowed the lump in his throat, moistened dry lips.

"You came," he whispered, thinking everything would be all right. Casey had finally arrived. The wedding could proceed. He frowned, realizing they weren't in the chapel. It didn't matter. Casey was there.

"Yes, I came," she said softly as she leaned closer. He felt her hand tremble in his, saw her green eyes turn to gold. A welcome warmth washed through his cold body as he remembered the other times her eyes had turned to gold—the first time he'd kissed her, the day he'd given her an Arabian colt the same color as her hair, the afternoon in her secret hideaway when they'd first made love.

He shivered, suddenly cold again, and an aching sense of loss seeped through him. Something had happened, he knew, but he couldn't remember what—only the loss and the longing.

"I—I was afraid . . . you wouldn't come," he said hoarsely.

Her smile faded, her eyes stopped glowing. "You needed me."

She turned her head away, but he heard her soft cry of distress. Damn. He shouldn't have told her about his fears . . . but he was so tired. Besides, Casey was his buddy. She had always understood how he felt. Hadn't she? Maybe she really *didn't* know how much she meant to him, he thought in panic. Had he ever told her he loved her? He couldn't remember. He would after the wedding. Finally.

He swallowed again and managed to say, "I waited so long."

Her image faded. He blinked his eyes, desperately trying to clear his vision; he never wanted to lose sight of Casey again. When the hazy veil passed, she was leaning over him once more. He could see the ripeness of her full, heart-shaped lips, smell the faint scent of the wildflower perfume she always wore. "But it was well worth the wait," he told her huskily. "You look lovely. So beautiful."

He felt himself slipping again and focused his gaze on her lips, remembering how sweet they tasted. It had been so long since he had kissed her. "Is it time yet to kiss the bride?" he asked hopefully.

Casey stared at Dare in dismay as his words rocked her to the core. He was remembering their wedding day! Suddenly she desperately wanted to kiss him, to ease his heartache as well as hers. Leaning over, she pressed her lips against his while her hot tears, held back for so long, won their release.

Her lips tasted just as sweet as he'd remembered, Dare thought as he sipped from them, fighting the waves of weakness that threatened to take him away. His lips were parched for her, his throat ached, and he continued to drink in her nectar like a man who was dying of thirst. It was heaven to kiss Casey again, and he tried to remember why he hadn't been in heaven for such a long time. It was his fault, he knew, but he was too tired to think about it now.

All he wanted to do was kiss Casey . . . and kiss her . . . and keep on kissing her until he no longer had any strength or breath left.

A massive pain hit him in the back, smashing the last of his strength, stealing his breath. What the hell was happening? Why was he so weak? So tired? Why did he feel as if he'd been blown through a derrick, then had plummeted back to the earth?

Another pain grabbed him, forcing a moan from his lips. Casey raised her head and gazed at him, tears streaming down her cheeks.

Why was she crying? Dare wondered in concern. Casey never cried. He tried to ask her but couldn't because the pain now had a death hold on his entire body, making it difficult to speak, to breathe, even to think. He gripped Casey's hand, struggling to control the pain, wanting to stay with Casey . . . wanting to remember . . . to remember.

Suddenly memory returned . . . and with it

the agony that had seared his soul the past three, lonesome, desolate years.

"You didn't come, did you, Casey?" he whispered as he closed his eyes and gave up his battle to stay with her. "You left me standing at the altar."

ONE

Dare picked up the phone, punched in the number of the Boone Blowout Control Company, then lay back on the hospital bed, holding the receiver against his ear.

"Yes, boss," Maureen answered.

"How did you know it was me?" Dare asked his office manager.

"Because no one else phones me every hour on the hour. I love you, big boy, but will you give me a break!"

Dare laughed softly. Maureen had a right to be miffed; he'd been bugging her constantly for the last two weeks. But, dammit, if he couldn't be at the office, he at least wanted to know what was going on. It was a habit that was hard to break. He'd been running the company for almost half of his life, since the day he'd become Cas Boone's partner, seventeen years before. Cas had been a lousy businessman, and at times he'd been a pain in the neck, but Dare had loved him. He missed him, would always miss him.

Tramping down hard on the memories, he spoke into the phone. "I'll keep this one brief, sweetheart. The next time Laramie reports in, tell him to bring home my tin box."

"Your tin box?" Maureen sounded as if he'd finally gone off the deep end. And she might have been right. If he'd been thinking clearly, he'd have remembered the box days earlier.

"Yeah, it's with my gear. Laramie will know what I mean."

"Don't you want the rest of your belongings?"

"They don't matter. Just make sure Laramie brings home the tin box."

Lord, he hoped it was safe, Dare thought as he hung up the receiver. He scrubbed his fingers through his hair, wishing he were back in Colombia rather than stuck in a damn hospital. Thank God none of the boys had been hurt.

He buried his face in his hands, telling himself that everything would be all right. Hadn't Casey promised him that he would walk again? She'd been standing beside him, holding his hand, when he'd woken up and realized he couldn't move his legs. Only her presence and her reassuring words had kept his panic at bay. He still couldn't move a muscle, but he clung to Casey's words because the alternative was unbearable.

Besides, he trusted Casey; she'd been his

shadow . . . his buddy since the day Madre had brought her home from the hospital because Casey's mother had been too ill to look after her. Cas couldn't afford to pay for nursing care, and Madre had brought Casey's mother home, too, saying it was the least she could do for her best friend. Eventually Cas had moved his family back to the adjacent Rocking R Ranch, but Casey had spent her first eight years living with the King family, bringing her special brand of sunshine into their lives—especially his.

Smiling at the memories, Dare reached over to the bedside stand and sliced a piece of Sin-City cake Casey had baked for him—the fourth cake she'd made him since he'd regained consciousness. He lay back on the pillows and slowly ate the rich strawberry-and-chocolate concoction, thinking that if he weren't careful, he'd be as fat as the Porky the Pig cartoon character painted on the opposite wall.

He'd been so doped up with painkillers, it had taken him a couple of days to realize he was in a children's hospital—Casey's idea. There was less chance the press—Billings in particular—would find him there. If the oil patch learned about his accident, everything he'd worked for could still go down the drain. Competition was fierce, and although the Boone Blowout Control Company was now in demand, he was afraid the phones would stop ringing if word got out that he couldn't walk —much less put out a fire.

Dammit all to hell, Dare thought, glaring at the wheelchair, which sat next to the bed. He had to get on his feet. Fast. There was too much at stake.

Suddenly the muggy, mid-September heat, which he'd been enjoying until then, became oppressive, and he threw off the top sheet. The happy sound of children's laughter drifted through the open window, intruding on his none-too-happy thoughts. He punched the button on the controls to raise the head of his bed, then looked down into the courtyard. Casey, dressed in green slacks and shirt, had just appeared and the kids were crowding around, demanding her attention. He'd spent hours watching her as she exercised their limbs, listening to the sound of her voice as she told them stories to keep their minds off their pain. He was particularly intrigued by the way she kept hugging one little boy, Billy Bob, although he tried to pretend he didn't want to be hugged. It was obvious the kid rated Casey right up there with chocolate ice cream—and that Casey thought the world of him.

Once he had dreamed of having children with Casey. Did she still want children? Dare wondered. Lowering the bed again, he turned his head away from the window and closed his eyes.

On her way off duty, Casey stopped in to say good night to Dare. He was sleeping, she realized as soon as she entered his room. And no wonder. Despite everything they'd done for him these past two weeks—the cold packs, hot packs, massages, and exercises—Dare was still suffering severe muscle spasms and excruciating pain. Yet, not once had he complained. In fact, they had to force the painkillers into him.

Quietly Casey crossed the room and gazed down at Dare, who was lying flat on his back, clad only in a pair of red boxer shorts, because he refused to wear a "damn sissy gown." He hadn't much liked the boxer shorts either, but had reluctantly agreed they were easier to put on. And after all the embarrassment she'd suffered buying them, he had better wear them, she thought. A grin tugged at the corner of her mouth as she wondered whether she'd ever get to tell him that story. Lord, how she missed telling Dare stories.

A sense of longing swept through her, and she tried to shake it off. It remained, settling in the lower half of her body, making her feel weak and . . . needy.

Dare looked so sexy, lying there, his bronzed arms crossed over his equally tanned chest, his long, powerful legs covered with thick, fine hair. No wonder the nurses had beat a path to his door the first few days—supposedly to sample the Sex-Between-the-Sheets cake she had baked for Dare, while the looks on their faces had made it very clear they really wanted to sample him. No wonder they still spent their coffee breaks talking about "the hunk with the shoulders that didn't stop," his pelt of curly chest hair they'd "just die" to run their fingers through. She doubted if they'd ever seen a man as big, as powerful, as ruggedly handsome as Dare, but their giggles and innuendos were making her mad. After all, Dare was hers.

No, he *wasn't* hers, she reminded herself sternly. Nor did she want him to be hers. Not if he was chasing around the world from one wild well to the next. And if, by chance, he could no longer fight those terrifying fires, she still wouldn't want him in her life. She had everything for which she dared to dream.

But for one weak, insane moment she longed to smooth his unruly hair off his forehead. To tease his full bottom lip with her finger. To see his warm, wonderful smile and know it was meant for her.

Slowly his long, curly lashes swept up, and he gazed at her, his brown eyes soft, unfocused. He blinked, then smiled, and suddenly she found herself wanting to dream again. Sadly she pushed the dreams aside.

"Hi," she whispered. "Sorry I woke you. I stopped in to say good-bye before I went home."

He continued to gaze at her, loving the sound of her sultry voice. It made him think of warm southern nights, satin sheets, and Casey, lying naked in his arms.

"I wasn't asleep," he drawled. "Just trying to relax and meditate."

"Is it working?"

"Nah, but it gives me something to do." He patted the bed. "Come, sit down a minute, princess."

"I shouldn't."

"You're off duty."

She gazed at him, knowing she would be breaking all sorts of regulations, but finding it difficult to refuse Dare's request. He had rarely asked her for anything, had always been the one to give to her.

Tentatively she settled one hip on the edge of the bed. He levered his torso over a bit, making room. She eased more of her weight onto the mattress, then stopped as she felt the warmth from his body through her thin cotton slacks. Shaken by the warmth, she drew in a deep breath and smelled the rich, tantalizing odor of sandalwood and spice, the scent she'd always associated with Dare.

Quickly, she looked away, her gaze resting on the cake she'd made for Dare. "Would you like some cake?" she asked, glancing back at him.

"I'll pass, thanks," he said, smiling at her, his brown eyes lingering on her face. "It's delicious, but I've just finished my third piece today. What are you trying to do, Casey? Fatten me up?"

"You could do with another thirty pounds." Mesmerized by his smile, she reached out and traced her fingertip along his rib cage where his cast had been.

He sucked in a startled gasp. She jerked her

finger back. Their gazes collided for a skip of a heartbeat, then each looked away; Dare at the window, Casey at the cake.

With a hand that trembled, she cut a generous slice of cake, then began eating it slowly, pinch by pinch.

Laughing softly, Dare turned his head to look at her. "Remember the first cake you made me? The Chocolate Volcano?"

Casey groaned, but her lips twitched and her eyes were full of laughter as she looked at him through lowered lashes. "You'll never let me live that one down, will you?"

"It exploded all over the oven."

"Because I used baking powder and self-rising flour." She giggled.

He chuckled. "I ate the whole thing, didn't I?"

"After you filled the crater with chocolate icing."

They laughed again, and Casey turned her attention back to the cake, feeling much more at ease than a few minutes before. Dare, the teasing big brother, she could handle. Dare, the lover—well, she hadn't had much experience with that side of the big, handsome man.

Lord, she was beautiful, Dare thought, watching her. Never in all his travels had he seen another woman with such gorgeous red hair, such dazzling eyes, such kissable lips. And never had he found a woman he wanted as much as he had wanted Casey.

He'd waited a long time for Casey to grow up, and three years earlier he had thought his wait was over. Then her father had been killed on their wedding day, and she had begged him to stop fighting fires.

Even now he could remember every word of their final conversation at the springs. . . .

"For years I've been telling myself that you live a charmed life, that nothing will happen to you," she had said, clutching at the lapels of the Spanish wedding jacket he wore. "That you will never leave me. But now I know better."

"Casey, I would never leave you."

She'd barely heard his reassurances. "All my life the people I've loved have left me. I won't wait around for you to leave me too."

"Casey, darlin'. What are you saying?"

She'd drawn away from him then, looking so lovely in her grandmother's wedding dress and veil, she'd made his heart ache. "That if you're going to keep fighting oil-well fires, *I don't want you in my life.*"

He would do anything in the world for Casey, but he couldn't quit—not then, not now. Not while he was still in hock to the bank. Lord, his life was an endless wasteland without Casey. The emptiness was almost too much to bear. Especially now that she was beside him once more.

"I was watching you with the kids," he said hoarsely, then cleared his throat. "You brighten up their days whenever you come near them."

Turning slightly, she looked at him as she wiped her fingers on a tissue. "I enjoy working with them very much," she said, poking the tissue into the paper bag taped on the over-bed table.

He reached out and took her hand. "Have I ever told you how proud I am of you? That you became a physical therapist."

His unexpected praise brought a lump to her throat, and she swallowed hard. "It's something I've always wanted to do, ever since I realized I could make Mama feel better by rubbing her legs."

"You were six at the time," Dare said thoughtfully, remembering the loving care Casey had given her mother . . . how sunny and cheerful she'd always been. How she'd never seemed to mind that she didn't have time to go out with the girls, or shop for clothes, or date boys. He wished he could have taken more of the load off her shoulders.

He gave her hand a careful squeeze as he continued, "I remember the look in your eyes when you told me in no uncertain terms that you were going to be 'sisio.' Even then I knew you'd do it. And that you'd be good at it. You have healing hands."

He also remembered those hands touching him in love, tentatively at first, then more boldly, making him ache with the need to bury himself inside her and find his release.

Suddenly Dare wanted . . . needed . . . Casey to touch him again. Not the way she'd been touching him these past two weeks—impersonally, as a therapist doing exercises on a patient—but as a woman in love.

Clamping down hard on his emotions, he released her hand before he did something unpardonable like kiss her.

"So, do you like working here?" he asked gruffly.

"I love it," she said, still glowing from his praise.

"It's obvious that everyone thinks the world of you." He frowned, recalling the way one handsome, young doctor looked at Casey. Dare didn't know what made him madder—the way Morton kept coming in to snitch some of *his* Sin-City cake, or the way he drooled over Casey if she happened to be in the room. "Especially that doctor, Miles Morton . . . the Third! Isn't it?"

Casey gave an embarrassed little laugh but said nothing. After a moment Dare continued, "So, what's the scoop on the Third?"

"We've dated occasionally," she said, keeping her gaze on her fingers as she picked at a piece of lint on the bottom sheet.

"Serious?"

"Dare!" She slid off the bed and glared down at him, one hand on her cocked hip. "I don't need you to vet my dates any longer."

He gave her a tight smile of apology. "That's right. You've built a new life for yourself, haven't you?"

"Yes, I have." The words sounded weak, even to her own ears, so she continued to speak, trying to bolster them up. "I have my ranch, my horses, my work with the children, and . . ." And she'd have to be content with that, Casey finished silently.

And another man, Dare finished for her. "Are you happy?" he asked, his eyes searching hers, demanding the truth, even though he wasn't sure he wanted to hear it.

She looked away, refusing to meet his gaze, despite the powerful pull of his eyes. "Yes, I am," she said, wondering if Dare was happy. She had a new life now without Dare, but what did he have? He didn't have a home of his own—not even an apartment in Houston. He didn't own an expensive sports car or a fast boat, and his wardrobe was very basic—work jeans and dress jeans. If the monthly checks she received from the company were any indication, Dare wasn't hurting for money. So why didn't he have any of the rich man's toys? she wondered, then answered her question. The only thing that was important to Dare was his family.

Suddenly Casey came to a decision she'd been agonizing over for the last two weeks. She didn't love Dare any longer, and Dare hadn't forgiven her for leaving him at the altar, but she was still part of his family. And family stuck together regardless of the risks, regardless of the costs. She'd vowed to help Dare walk again, and she was going to keep that vow, despite the fact that it would mean letting him back into her life.

It would only be for a short time, she reassured herself as she looked up at him again. Should she tell him about her plans? she wondered, then decided against it.

"Then I'm happy for you," Dare said softly, breaking in on her thoughts.

He *was* happy for Casey, he told himself again a few minutes later as he watched the door close behind her. Casey deserved to be happy. She didn't need to be tied down to an old crock like him.

The door opened again, and he smiled, wondering if Casey had forgotten something. His smile fled as a grim looking Dr. Bell entered the room.

TWO

At ten that evening, Casey once again entered Dare's room, summoned by the head nurse to "talk some sense into the hunk's thick skull." Although racked with sever pain, he was adamantly refusing an analgesic, and nothing else they'd tried had helped.

Casey paused in the doorway, knowing immediately that something else was bothering Dare; his special smile was missing, his rugged features were bleak and hard.

He lay there, naked except for his shorts, his arms folded over his chest, grimly watching her as she crossed the room. "You lied to me," he accused the moment she reached the bed.

"King! I have never, ever, lied to you," she said, surprised by his attack. "So what put that bee in your bonnet?"

"Bell just told me I'll never walk again," he

said, turning his head away from Casey and the concern in her emerald eyes—the concern she'd been valiantly trying to hide for the last two weeks. Now he knew the reason why.

Casey stared at Dare in dismay. Why in the dickens did Bell have to shoot off his mouth so fast? Why couldn't he have kept the bad news until Dare was in better shape to hear it? Then she remembered two things she'd seen happen time and time again when Dr. Bell had talked to patients or their parents. He always held out hope, no matter how severe the injury; however, the patient never heard the hope, only the bad news.

"You must be mistaken," she told Dare firmly. "Dr. Bell would *never* say anything like that."

"I wouldn't walk up to a burning well given the odds he quoted." Bell's words had also reinforced the fear that had been riding his shoulders since he'd realized he couldn't move his legs.

But then he'd carried the fear around most of his life, he admitted as he rolled his head back and gazed at Casey, his eyes turning soft and tender with memories. Ever since the year he'd spent in bed with a broken back. The year Casey was born.

"So are you going to give up?" she asked, even though she already knew the answer. Dare would never give up.

"No way." Even saying the words made him feel better. He'd faced tremendous odds in the past, had taken calculated risks, and had always won—except when he'd lost Casey.

"Good. Neither am I. I hate to work with a patient who has given up."

"Is that all I am to you, a patient?" he asked quietly, his gaze lingering on her face.

Heaven help her, Casey thought, it was no different than it had been in the past. All Dare had to do was look at her with his chocolate eyes, and she felt like melting on the spot.

"It's better this way," she told him, warning herself that she *had better* treat him like a patient or she'd never pull off the plan she'd already put in action. Duke had moved Dare's clothes into her house—into her bedroom, in fact. Now all she had to do was convince Dare to come home with her. But that might be impossible, considering the way they had parted three years before. She sighed, then added huskily, "Because you're going to hate me before we're through."

"Princess . . . I would never hate you."

Even his deep, gravelly voice had a way of turning her bones into marshmallows, and for a moment she considered changing her plans. But hadn't she just decided to help Dare, no matter what it might cost her?

"Remember that when your muscles are screaming with pain and I'm demanding that you do more," she muttered as she shoved her fingers through her hair, holding it up over her ear.

He caught back a groan as he watched her, knowing her provocative gesture was totally unintentional. She was so damn sexy, and if he was feeling any better, he'd be a hell of a lot more than a patient to her. "Well, it's a moot point, Casey, because I don't plan to hang around here and let you torture me. I want out. Immediately."

"That's no surprise. What's surprising is that you've waited this long to make your demands." She let her hair fall in a curtain over her eyes, and kept them downcast, fixed on the toes of her boots. "So, where do you want to go? Home?"

Dare clamped his jaw tightly. He wanted to go home so badly, he ached. "Madre has her work cut out for her, looking after the Baron since his stroke. Can you see my father and me, two cripples, confined in the same house?"

Her head shot up and she glared at him. "Darrick King, you are not a cripple, and I *never* want to hear you say that word again."

"Well, I can't move my legs," he pointed out, a wry smile touching his lips but not making it to his eyes.

"*Can't* is another word I don't want to hear from you." Deliberately she reached over and dug her fingers hard into his thigh muscle. "You can feel that, can't you?"

"Yeah."

"And you'll move your legs, too, Dare. You just need time to heal. Time and therapy."

Maybe she was right. Maybe he would walk again, Dare thought, wanting desperately to believe Casey rather than that damn doctor. He tried to lift his leg, tried to press it against Casey's hand. It wouldn't move.

"How long?" he demanded as he tried again.

"Dare! Don't push so hard," Casey cried out. His stubborn determination had brought him a long way in such a short time, but she wished he wasn't so impatient. "It might be months before you can walk again."

"No damn way it'll take that long," he said through teeth gritted in determination.

She shook her head, thinking she might as well wish for the moon to stop shining. Dare would push himself to the limits if she let him. Deliberately taking matters into her own hands, she clasped his knee, raised it off the bed, then pressed it back into the mattress. With a muttered curse he flopped back and stared at the ceiling.

She began massaging his thigh, telling herself that she was trying to ease his pain, warning herself to be impersonal. It was totally impossible. The moment she felt his firm, hair-roughened skin, her body began quivering, her heart began pounding erratically, and she could barely breathe.

Heavens to Betsy! This had happened every time she'd touched Dare these past two weeks. It was a miracle she hadn't turned into a bowl of jelly by now. She concentrated on her fingers, willing them to behave, to forget they had once known him . . . to get on with their job. After a few minutes her training came to the rescue and she was able to pretend, once more, that Dare was just a patient.

Dare groaned in relief as her kneading fingers began to ease the cramp from his muscles. "Why is it that you can take away the pain when nothing I do seems to touch it?"

She risked looking at him again. "I don't know, Dare, but I'm glad it works." He was still frowning, she noted, and redoubled her efforts. "You have to learn to relax, Dare. Take a deep breath in and blow it out slowly. Breathe in and out. Think of a cool—"

"I can't go home. I don't want the folks to see me like this," he said, remembering how much his mother had agonized over him the year he'd spent in bed. He'd never put her through that again.

"Then where do you want to go? A rehab center? Another hospital?"

That was the major hitch, Dare admitted silently. He had nowhere else to go, especially when he didn't have two bucks to rub together and Billings had been hounding him since their little altercation three years earlier. "The press is sure to find out what happened to me if I check into another hospital. It's a miracle someone hasn't already leaked the news."

"I've called in a few favors," she said, glancing up again to give him a shy smile.

Dare couldn't help but smile back. That was just like his buddy. Always trying to protect him, despite the fact that he was six inches taller and over a hundred pounds heavier than she was . . . and had never once needed her protection.

"But you're right about the press finding out if you go anywhere else. You're a national hero, especially in these parts," she continued, her voice as mellow as old wine. "So how about coming home with me?"

"Home?"

"To the Rocking R."

Ah, the Rocking R, Dare thought, squelching the longing that rose inside him again. Casey's ranch now, but at what a cost. "I can't go there."

"Why not?" she asked, carefully keeping her eyes on her fingers, which were still massaging his leg. "It would be a perfect place for you to recuperate, thanks to the renovations your mother made so Mama could stay at home."

He shook his head, thinking that fate had a way of messing up a man's plans. Fate and—if he were honest about it—a man's folly. He sighed, then caught his breath as a sharp pain erupted through his back and down into his legs.

Casey glanced up, her eyes shining with concern. "Dare! Is it bad?"

"A real blowout." He tried to smile, but gave it up as another pain tore through him. Perspiration beaded his forehead and dotted his upper lip.

"I'll ring for some pain pills."

"No pills," he grated out through clenched teeth.

"Dare—"

"I'm not taking any more of them." He squeezed his eyes shut, trying to force the pain back into its hole and put a cap on it. "And I don't want you to look after me."

With a sigh she turned away, caught up a towel from the bedside stand, and began wiping the perspiration off his face. "I won't be looking after you, Dare," she said, struggling to keep her voice calm and reasonable. "You'll be looking after yourself. All I'll be doing is helping you with your physical therapy."

"What about your job?" he asked, trying to remember all the reasons why he shouldn't go home with her.

"I'll take a leave of absence."

"What about the children? You just finished telling me how much you enjoy looking after them."

Helplessly she gazed down at him, watching the struggle he was waging with the pain. Why wouldn't he give in and ask for some analgesic? More to the point, why wouldn't he give in and come home with her? Was it because he was such a proud, stubborn man? Or was it because he still hadn't forgiven her? "It will only be for a little while, Dare," she said softly. "Until you're on your feet again."

He opened his eyes. "I won't be a burden on you, princess," he whispered hoarsely.

Her throat was suddenly so tight, she could

barely force the words out. "You'd *never* be a burden."

He shook his head. "You spent most of the first eighteen years of your life looking after your mother. You never had time for friends or fun. I don't want you to have to look after me too."

"Dare, for heaven's sake!" Placing her hands along his whiskered jaw, she gazed deeply into his brown eyes. They were dark with pain, but also warm with . . . concern, she realized, her heart turning over in a slow loop. Concern for her. Her lips quivered, and she pressed them together, striving for control. "I've already told you that I won't be looking after you," she finally managed, her voice husky.

Catching her hands in his, he pulled them away from his face, then released them. "And I'm telling you for the last time. *No.*"

Hands on hips, she stared down at him, her eyes glistening with tears. "Now you listen up, King, and listen good. You've done so much for me, given me so much, I'll be in your debt forever. Why won't you let me do something for you?"

Her tears made Dare feel lower than a hog's belly for hurting her, and he ached to reach out and comfort her. "As far as I'm concerned, you wiped out all your debts—" He sucked in a deep breath as another pain shot through his legs. He closed his eyes and instead of reaching for her, clenched his hands into white-knuckled fists at his side.

The day I left you standing at the altar, Casey finished the sentence for him, feeling so hopeless. Dare was never going to forgive her.

Turning away, she walked over to the window and rested her forehead against the cool glass. What a mess they'd made of it all. Dare was such a proud man, such a shy, private man. And because of her own pride and stubbornness, Dare had been embarrassed in front of his family and friends at the chapel. Then, thanks to Fred Billings, the reporter of a national tabloid, Dare had been held up to shame and ridicule to the whole country. DISTRAUGHT BRIDE LEAVES DAREDEVIL STANDING AT THE ALTAR, the headlines had read, followed by an equally damaging KING RESPONSIBLE FOR HER FATHER'S DEATH.

If only she hadn't insisted on waiting alone in the vestibule of the small, family chapel on the Regent Ranch for her father to arrive in time to walk her down the aisle. If only she hadn't refused Duke and Dev's offer to hang around "just in case." If only she had let Madre King, the woman who had been a mother to her, stay with her.

Instead, she had clung to her belief that, for once, her father would be with her for an important event in her life. Dare had arrived early that morning, flying halfway across the world from the gas fields in Algeria to be there for the wedding. Her father only had to drive in from a blowout in West Texas. Surely he would arrive in time, she had told herself, and had insisted the organist begin playing the wedding march on the stroke of two.

The phone in the vestibule had rung at four minutes to two, and she'd picked up the receiver, thinking it was her father calling to say he'd be a few minutes late. Instead Fred Billings had asked her to comment on her father's death, then informed her of the horrifying details.

She had run from the chapel, run from Dare, leaving him to face the music alone.

Casey brushed the tears from her cheeks with the sides of her hands, remembering how he'd looked at the wedding—thanks to the home video her friend had taken and which Casey had played over and over again until every second was permanently engraved in her mind . . . so big and virile and at ease, despite the Spanish wedding clothes he'd worn at her request. How he turned, with the first chords of the wedding march, and looked toward the back of the chapel, smiling expectantly with that soft, sexy, special smile he reserved only for her. His smile faded, replaced by a frown of concern as the march ended. With a wave of his hand he gestured his two brothers to stay put, then strode down the aisle, unmindful of the murmurs and stares of the congregation, and disappeared into the vestibule. Seconds later he walked back into the chapel.

"I'm sorry, friends," he said quietly and with great dignity. "But it appears as if Casey has had second thoughts about getting married. I don't know what the problem is, but I'm sure y'all will give Casey your love and understanding, now and in the future." He sent a special smile up the aisle in the direction of his mother. "Madre has been cooking up a storm for weeks, so why don't y'all go on up to the house and eat while I go see what has happened to Casey."

She could only guess at how much it had cost the proud man to say those words, because never once had he raised his voice in anger. Not even when he'd found her in her secret hideaway at the springs.

She'd been numb with shock, and so desperately afraid Dare would also leave her that she couldn't remember what she'd said. Except that she'd begged him to quit fighting fires, and when he'd refused, she had told him to stay out of her life.

Maybe she should give up on the idea of helping Dare, she thought, then squared her shoulders. No, she wouldn't give up on Dare. Not until *he told her* that he didn't want her in his life.

Dammit, Dare thought, still struggling with the pain. He wished he could go home with Casey. What he wouldn't give to breathe fresh air again . . . to feel the heat of the sun again. To be with Casey again. He opened his eyes, blinked away the haze, and saw Casey standing by the window.

"What's the matter, Casey?" he asked, his voice gruff.

She swung around but remained by the window. "You can't forgive me, can you, Dare?" she blurted out, then added softly, "Not that I blame you."

Bewildered, he shook his head. "What are you talking about?"

"You can't forgive me for leaving you at the altar, can you?" she said, giving him a sad little smile. "That's the reason you won't come home with me."

His jaw dropped open in surprise. "Lord, no, Casey! The thought never entered my head." The pain-etched lines at the corners of his eyes became softer, and his voice grew deeper as he continued, "I told you, Casey, the only reason I don't want to go home with you is that I don't want to be a burden on you."

"Friends are never burdens, Dare. But I guess I'm no longer your friend."

"Casey." He held out his hand. "Come here, princess."

Slowly she approached the bed and placed her hand in his. He held it, brushing his thumb gently over her knuckles, gazing into her eyes. "I also told you, Casey, that I would always be your friend, no matter what," he said softly.

Regardless of the fact that she didn't want to be his buddy anymore, he added silently. He couldn't blame her for feeling that way; he had only himself to blame for what had happened . . . to Cas. To Casey. To the two of them.

The compassion, the honest-to-goodness caring in Dare's eyes gave her hope. The plaster that had encased her heart for the last three years slowly began to crumble. "I'm sorry, Dare, for embarrassing you in front of your family and friends," she whispered, then still needing to hear the words from him, she added, "Can you ever forgive me?"

THREE

Forgive her, Dare thought in disbelief. If he could, he'd get down on his hands and knees and—

He choked back the words that sprang from the depths of his soul. "Casey, there's nothing to forgive. You'd just learned about your father's death. No wonder you couldn't go through with the wedding."

"You mean you haven't been angry with me all these years?"

He raised her hand to his lips and brushed a kiss across her knuckles. "I have never, ever, been angry with you, Casey."

His words and his featherlight kiss sent a shiver of wonder through her, and it was a moment before she could manage a bewildered, "Then why have you been avoiding me?"

He kept his gaze on her knuckles. "I've been busy, you know."

Know. She couldn't help but know. She shivered again, remembering the apprehension she'd felt every time she'd seen his face on the cover of a magazine, or read his name in the headlines—first during the hellfires of Kuwait, then as the *Daredevil* and his team capped one impossible well after another. Thank God she didn't have to worry about turning on the TV and learning of Dare's death. Until he was back on his feet again.

Deliberately she forced the thought and the worry aside. "You were never too busy before," she reminded him. "So what was the real reason?"

Slowly he raised his gaze to hers. "Because you told me to stay away. Remember?"

Her eyes turned dark green with distress. "Yes . . . I remember, but I never thought you'd take my words so literally. You've always been there on the fringes of my life, if not the center, and I thought . . . oh, never mind."

"I'm sorry, Casey." He soothed his callused thumb over her knuckles. "I thought it would be better if I stayed completely away. I couldn't give you what you wanted . . . I couldn't quit fighting oil-well fires, and I thought it would be easier on you, that you wouldn't . . . worry so much if I wasn't around." He'd also come to the gut-wrenching conclusion that she still held him responsible for her father's death. Otherwise she would have contacted him, or at least sent him a heart.

"Not worry! Hah! I worried."

"I'm sorry," he repeated, not knowing what else to say.

She eased her hand out of his and immediately felt the loss of its warmth and strength, just as she had felt the loss of his warmth and strength when he hadn't been part of her life. "But you didn't even attend the family gatherings, and you always enjoyed them so much."

"So did you, and I was afraid you wouldn't go if I was there."

Casey gazed at him, shaking her head. Dare had a heart as big as the rest of him, she thought, tears burning the back of her eyes. She blinked quickly and managed a smile. "Oh, Dare. Dare. You've done it again. You've been taking care of me and my needs at the expense of your own happiness. Please, please let me do something for you."

"Nothing's changed, Casey," he said quietly. "As soon as I can walk again, I have to go back to fighting fires."

"I . . . I know." But she wouldn't think about that now, not when he needed her.

"And I don't want to hurt you, princess."

"The only thing that will hurt me is if you refuse to let me help you."

He stared at her for a long moment, knowing that in spite of everything she had said, he should still refuse. But he couldn't. Not when it obviously meant so much to Casey. "All right. I'll go home with you."

She smiled at him, a wide, sunny smile full of relief. "Thank you."

"But only if you promise that I won't interfere with your social activities. Dating the Third. Going out with the girls. Whatever."

"I haven't been going out very often."

"Casey!"

"Okay, I promise."

"And only for a month."

"Six," she bargained, then seeing his frown, quickly added, "If you need that much time."

"Two at the most." He clenched his jaw together as another massive pain gripped him. Finally it eased enough so he could continue. "I'll stay until Thanksgiving, then I'll get out of your life, even if I have to crawl."

He would do just that, Casey thought as she began massaging his legs again, coaching him to relax with her soothing words, leading him to a place far away, where it was safe and free from pain. This brave, strong, stubborn man would disappear from her life if he thought for one second that he was going to be a burden on her. So she was going to have to be extremely careful. As much as she would love to wait on him hand and foot, she was going to have to let him be as independent as possible. Which meant, she suspected, that he would soon be insisting on taking care of her.

The one thing she had learned in the last three years was that she could survive without Dare's help. Dare was going to have to learn that too.

Gradually she felt his body relax and knew the worst of his pain was over. Glancing up at him, she saw that he was still awake—but just barely. His eyes were heavy-lidded, a boyish smile softened his lips.

"What did you mean a little while ago?" she asked. "About me wiping out all my debts?"

His smile grew softer, warmer, more intimate, but he lost the battle to keep his eyes open. "You wiped out all your debts, princess," he said, his voice deep and low, "the day you were born."

Then before she could ask him what he meant, he drifted off to sleep.

Dare lay with his eyes closed, listening to the sound that had wakened him. A mockingbird greeting the new day. Once he had greeted each new day with joy, but he hadn't felt that way for a long time. Three years and counting. Every since Casey had learned that her bigger-than-life hero had feet of clay.

Now he was lying in her bed . . . knowing he would give his soul if he could be her hero again.

But that would never happen. Even if he could walk again, there were too many obstacles in the way. Too many things he'd done and hadn't done. Too many words that had been spoken and words that had not been said. There was no chance on God's green earth that Casey and he would have a future together, especially when Casey was building a future without him.

He shouldn't have come home with her, he thought, then sighed as the mockingbird sang again. If the truth be known, he was relieved. He didn't want to go home, and he had nowhere else to go.

Besides, the Rocking R had been a second home since the day Cas had insisted on moving his family back to the ranch, which had been in his wife's family for generations. Dare had accompanied them, and while Madre had settled Elise into her bedroom he'd taken Casey exploring through the rambling hacienda, pointing out its thick walls, red-tiled roof, and cool, secluded courtyard. When her sunny face had threatened to cloud up, he'd helped her saddle her pony and taken her to the springs. This would be her special place, he'd told her, where she could come when she was happy or sad or just needed to get away for a while.

"But I don't want to leave you," she'd cried, clinging to his waist.

He knelt down beside her, took one of her hands, and placed it on his shirt above his heart, then placed his hand against her chest. "Do you know what this means?" he'd asked, feeling her heart pounding beneath his fingers. She shook her head, watching him solemnly with her big green eyes. "It means we're buddies now." He smiled as her pretty little face lit up. "And buddies never leave each other."

From that day on, he'd stopped by to visit his buddy whenever he was at home. The ranch house and springs held a lot of memories. . . . Such as the day of her fifteenth birthday when he'd given her Sundancer. And her sixteenth birthday when he'd given Casey her first kiss. And the day Cas had sold the ranch to buy the condo in Houston for his wife. Seventeen-year-old Casey had been heartbroken, and only Dare's promise to let her keep Sundancer at the Regent Ranch had dried her tears. Thank goodness, Casey was back on her ranch again.

Opening his eyes, Dare looked around the bedroom he'd once hoped to share with Casey, noting the changes she'd made since she'd moved back home: the fresh coat of apricot paint on the walls, the cherry-wood furniture, and the peach-and-plum curtains that matched the spread and sheet he'd thrown off the king-size brass bed.

Dressed in costumes from around the world, the dolls he'd given her over the years were arranged around the room. Some were on the window seat. Others were propped on the floor. Still more dolls were attending a tea party around the child-size table and chairs he'd made Casey one Christmas. Seated in the place of honor—a tiny rocker—was the first doll he'd given her. A princess for a princess. He smiled, remembering Casey's face the evening she'd opened the present, and how she had packed the doll around the house.

Would she let her children play with the dolls? Dare wondered. Was that why she had kept them?

And who was going to be the father of her children? Miles Morton the Third?

The thought lay like sour milk on his stomach. He swallowed the rancid taste, then tried to sit up. His leg muscles cramped in protest, becoming hard knots. He flopped back onto the bed. He took a deep breath. He tried to relax. Relief did not come, and he reached up and gripped the brass rungs above his head.

He took another deep breath, trying to visualize—the way Casey had taught him—a safe place where the pain couldn't get him. A place like Casey's hideaway, so cool and green and silent, except for the gurgle of the springs, the song of the mockingbird . . . and the breathy little sounds Casey had made when she'd given herself to him . . . with love.

"Dare . . . Dare, are you all right?"

Slowly he opened his eyes, and found himself in bed with Casey gazing down at him in concern —not love.

He smiled. "Yeah, just dandy."

Casey stared down at Dare, her mouth suddenly flooding with saliva. He was sprawled out on her bed, his arms curled above his head, naked except for a pair of black boxer shorts. His thick, brown hair was tumbled over his forehead, his face was flushed, his dark brown eyes heavy-lidded and sexy, almost as if he had been making love.

He was the reason why she'd bought a king-size bed instead of a queen, she suddenly realized as a warm, quivery feeling invaded her entire body. Dare was no longer part of her life, but subconsciously she must have been hoping he would be. She stepped back, ordered her heart to stop hammering, her stomach to stop knocking at her throat, and her eyes to stop devouring Dare as if he were a piece of rum-spice cake. Dare was a patient, not her lover.

"Good," she said, then swallowed hard. "I thought I heard you call out." She'd lain awake most of the night, very aware of Dare sleeping in the next room, listening intently in case he needed her. He hadn't called out, but she'd come into his room anyway, drawn by her own need to make sure he was all right.

"Nope. I was lying here thinking about getting dressed." Sleepily he let his gaze linger, noting the sunbeams dancing in her red curls, the gold sparkles in her bright green eyes. His gaze drifted lower. His fingers itched to touch her. Her white shirt was knotted below her rounded breasts, leaving her trim tummy exposed. Her jeans were cut off so short, they left little of her firm, honey-colored thighs to the imagination.

He licked his dry lips, swallowed hard. "From the looks of you, we won't be formal today," he said when he finally found his tongue.

The look in his eyes made her back up another step. It also made her wonder if she should hightail it out of his room while she still had the strength to walk. "It's going to be hot, so wear your trunks," she said, trying to take charge of the situation. "After breakfast, we'll do some exercises in the pool."

Still disconcerted by the expression in his eyes, she leaned over to pick up the book he'd been reading the night before.

Dare's gaze followed the long, sleek lines of her legs. Those legs had always held promise—a promise they had fulfilled magnificently, in that cool, green hideaway.

Desire suddenly surged to his loins, filling him so full, he was hard and hot with need, making him ache to pull her down on the bed and bury himself so deep inside her that he'd get lost. His knuckles turned white as he gripped the rails. Slowly he opened his hands and lowered his arms to his sides.

Unable to keep her eyes off Dare, Casey watched, admiring the muscle groups in his wide shoulders, his broad chest, and his powerful arms. Muscles that didn't bulge but rippled. Muscles he'd built up through years of hard work—not pumping iron. She had seen Dare effortlessly guide a "Christmas tree" onto a wellhead . . . and she had felt those very same arms holding her while his big hands had touched her gently . . . the afternoon they'd made love at the springs.

She squeezed her eyes shut, trying to banish the images. When she opened them, she saw the rails on the bedstead. It was made of antique brass and was so heavy it had taken two men to carry it into the bedroom. The two rails he'd been gripping were now bowed at the center.

She cried out, pressed her fingers to her lips, and gazed at him, her eyes betraying her concern. Dare glared at her, silently warning her not to say one word.

"I—I thought we'd get an early start on the exercises," she blurted out. Moving to the end of the bed, she picked up the spread and sheet and put them on the chair.

"You're going to do them here? In bed?"

She definitely was courting trouble, but she wasn't about to back down. "It'll be easier when you haven't started to tense up yet. When you're still relaxed and hanging loose because you've been asleep," she said as she began exercising his leg.

He snorted. "Relaxed. Hanging loose. Those aren't exactly the words I'd use to describe my present condition." But this kind of discomfort he could handle, he thought, silently acknowledging his relief. The possibility of being impotent had been as depressing as the possibility of not walking.

She glanced at his pelvis, then away quickly as she realized that Dare was also reacting to their more intimate circumstances. This had never happened in the hospital. A blush heated her cheeks and her fingers shook. She dug them into the muscle of his leg, attacking it as though it were full of demons.

Dare watched, a wicked grin on his lips. "With six other bedrooms in the house, why am I using yours?" he drawled.

"It's the only one that's wheelchair accessible," she muttered, trying to concentrate on his legs.

"Life is kinda ironic, isn't it," he said slowly. "I waited for years to get into your bed, but I always thought that when it happened you'd be lying beside me. Naked."

Her eyes, wide with shock, swept up to meet his. "Darrick King! Are you trying to fluster me?"

"Me, fluster you?" He cocked his head, looking at her innocently. "Now, why would I want to do that?"

"Because you're lying there feeling helpless and frustrated, and you want to prove you're macho." To prove that she wasn't flustered, she deliberately looked at his pelvis, then quickly averted her gaze again. The hard ridge of flesh, which lay beneath the black boxer shorts, was still big enough to make her legs tremble and her heart tap wildly. Think of something cold and relaxing, she ordered herself—but for the life of her she couldn't think of one single, solitary thing except Dare, and how he'd made her feel when they'd made love.

Taking a deep breath, she lowered his right leg to the bed, then quickly began exercising his left.

He laughed softly. "So, what do you think, Casey? Give me your honest opinion. Am I macho?"

She rolled her eyes to the ceiling, blew a strand of hair off her nose, then met his amused gaze. "I know you don't give a hoot whether anyone thinks you're macho, King. Just as I know you're a man of very few words, so don't try and play lover boy with me."

Yes, Casey knew him well. Too damn well, Dare thought, turning his head away so she couldn't see his eyes. "If I remember correctly, I *did* talk to you when you were in college," he said softly. "Almost every week, even if I had to phone you from some of the most remote places in the world."

"Yes, you did phone, Dare, but I did most of the talking. It is something I'll always be grateful to you for. You helped me get through my first big exam, my first day on the wards, the night my first patient died. You were there for me, Dare, even though you were thousands of miles away."

No wonder she had fallen in love with Dare, Casey thought as she gave his legs a final rub. Not only was he knock-them-dead handsome, he was also one of the most sensitive, caring men she had ever met. Finished with the exercise, she moved to his side.

He rolled his head back, and she smiled at him. "So, yes, I do know you, King," she continued, wagging a finger. "And I won't let you frighten me off with sexy innuendos."

"I guess I'm the one who has a lot to learn about you, Casey," he said thoughtfully. "You've changed. You're more self-assured. You're no longer the shy, young maiden who had to be told a hundred times she was beautiful, and still didn't believe it."

Demurely she lowered her lashes. "You're right. I'm no longer a young maiden."

He sucked in a sharp breath, and she looked up to find his brown eyes full of guilt. "I'm sorry, Dare. I didn't mean that the way it sounded," she said, wondering—as she had done many times in the past—if Dare had asked her to marry him because he felt guilty for making love to her. He had certainly insisted on a short engagement—which had been fine and dandy with her. She had almost given up hope that he'd ever ask her to marry him.

His gaze softened and a smile touched his lips. "But you're still beautiful, Casey," he said huskily. "More beautiful now than before—if that's possible."

She laughed self-consciously. "And you're still very good for my ego. But flattery won't get you anywhere with me, big boy. Move your bones. We have work to do."

Work! Hell, he should be down in Colombia capping that well, not flat on his back in bed, Dare thought in frustration, remembering the million other things he should be doing. "Before you start torturing me, I have to phone the office and see how things are going."

Casey paused at the door and looked back at him. "Maureen phoned last night and threatened to quit if you called her once more. You're driving her bonkers! However, since she's such a sweet, loyal employee, she'll phone you once a day and let you know what's going on."

"But—"

"I wouldn't cross her, Dare. She sounded as if she meant business, and you know how much you need her to keep you in line."

"Hmmph. Seems to me there's more'n one person in these parts who's keeping me in line."

"No arguments. You're here to learn how to walk, and you can't do that if you have a phone growing out of your ear. The company will survive without you."

Lord, he hoped so, Dare thought. To have come this far and then lose everything because he'd been hurt. He couldn't let that happen—especially when it would also affect Casey.

"I'll go and make breakfast while you get dressed," Casey said, wondering why Dare was looking so tense and strained. And because he was still frowning, she attempted to lighten the mood. "Remember to wear your trunks. I'm not through torturing you yet."

FOUR

Torture was a mild word for what he was suffering, Dare thought a few hours later as he watched Casey walk past him down the steps into the pool. Torture had been the humiliation of having to drag himself from the blasted wheelchair to the edge of the pool backward, on his butt, because it was either that or let Casey lower him into the water in the lift he'd made years ago for her mother. Torture was having to sit on the steps in the shallow end when he ached to swim laps.

But that was nothing compared with the sheer gut-wrenching agony of seeing Casey dressed in a green-and-blue bathing suit that clung to her full breasts and her tiny waist—and was cut high over her hips. Of wanting her so badly he was afraid he would burst, and wondering how the hell he was going to get through the next hour without doing something about it.

The agony had only begun, he realized a moment later when Miles Morton the Third entered the courtyard through the arched gate at the side of the house.

"Casey, I thought I'd find you out here," Miles called as he began walking toward them, weaving around the orange trees, rosebushes, and other shrubbery that made the courtyard so cool and inviting.

Casey swung her sleek body up onto the lip of the pool, stood, and waved. "Miles. What a pleasant surprise."

Dare watched, mesmerized, as droplets of water trickled down her throat, traveled along the ripe, round curves of her breasts, and disappeared into the deep cleft between them. More beads of water merged and meandered down her smooth legs, while others clung to the insides of her thighs. Lord, how he ached to follow the water with his fingers, his lips.

Just as he ached to punch Morton in the nose, he decided as the handsome, blond-headed doctor reached the pool. How dare Morton ogle his Casey.

Morton, dressed in a navy silk shirt and immaculately pressed white cotton slacks, stared at Casey as though thunderstruck. "Ah, hello, Casey." He spared Dare a glance. "King," he said tersely, then returned his gaze to Casey. "Ah, Casey, dear, don't you think that . . . ah, bathing suit is a trifle too brief to be wearing when you're working with a patient?"

Casey glanced down at her bathing suit in confusion. What was the big deal? It covered her adequately. She often wore it when she was working with the children. "Dare's seen me in this old thing a dozen times."

"And I like it," Dare put in, lying through his teeth. He loved it, but he sure as hell wished Morton couldn't see so much of Casey's lovely body.

Morton rubbed a bent finger across his trim mustache. "Well, it doesn't seem appropriate, my dear. And I don't think you should be looking after King either."

"What do you mean?" Casey asked, frowning in puzzlement.

"I think, and Mother agrees, that it isn't appropriate for a single woman to be looking after a single man, day in and day out. It's all right if you're in a hospital setting, I guess, but not in your home. It's an imposition."

"Just a minute, now. Let me get this straight." Casey straightened her back, drew herself up to her full height—just shy of six feet—which matched Morton's. "You think it's all right for me to look after Dare in the hospital because there are other people around to keep things on the up-and-up, but it isn't *proper* to look after him here. What's the matter? Do you think I'll take advantage of him?"

"For heaven's sake, no." Morton reached out

to touch Casey's shoulder, hesitated, then dropped his hand to his side. "I'm concerned he'll take advantage of you."

"Dare would never do that," Casey said staunchly.

Dare passed a hand over his face, covering his wide grin. Casey, his beloved buddy, was doing it again. Charging to his defense, whereas, if she only knew how he was really feeling, she'd be tearing a strip off his back. "I think what y'all are missing here is trust," Dare drawled as he laid his arm up along the edge of the pool. "And it seems to me that trust is a prerequisite of any meaningful relationship."

Morton planted his feet and looked down at Dare. "I trust Casey. It's you I don't trust. After all, you were engaged to her once."

"And Casey decided I wasn't the man for her." Dare lifted his hand and slowly clenched his fist. "But let me give you a tip, Morton. If she decides you're the man for her, you had better treat her right. Or you'll have me to answer to."

Casey stared in amazement at the two men who were fighting—*fighting*—over her. True, she had gone out with Miles a few times, but he was so mild-mannered, she didn't think he had a jealous bone in his body. Why had he come out to the ranch today? To warn Dare off his turf? To stake a claim?

And Dare. Why was he acting so protective?

She was grown up now. She didn't need him checking out her dates.

The whole thing was absolutely ridiculous.

"Look, Miles, I'm sure you didn't come out here to comment on my bathing suit," she said, wishing Miles wasn't so conservative. But that was one of the reasons she'd agreed to date him, she reminded herself. Miles was safe.

"No, I came to get the therapy plan for the little Dawson girl. Bell said you were working on it at home."

"I'll go get it. Do you want to come into the house for a glass of iced tea or something?" she asked, hoping to separate the men. Not that Miles would hit a man when he was down. Although Dare was at an extreme disadvantage, he wouldn't need any protection if it came to blows. He was still powerful enough to win any encounter with one hand tied behind his back.

Morton's gaze lingered on Casey's curves as he slowly shook his head. "Thanks, but I'll stay out here."

"Dare, will you be okay?" Casey asked, reluctant to leave.

"I'll keep hanging on, darlin'."

After giving the two men another anxious look, she hurried across the courtyard into the house.

Dare watched her, admiring the graceful way she moved and her cute little wiggle. "She's quite the gal," he said when she'd disappeared into the house.

"You can say that again."

"So what are your intentions toward her?" Dare drawled.

Morton, who had also been watching Casey, snapped his head around to look at Dare. "What business is it of yours?"

"Well, outside of the fact that I *did* ask her to marry me, Casey is also family, has been family since the day she was born."

Morton rubbed his mustache again. "Kind of kinky, wasn't it, asking a woman to marry you when she was almost a sister?"

"Casey stopped being a sister a long time ago. But I'd give her my dying breath, if she needed it." Dare's level gaze searched Morton's face. "So, what are your intentions?"

"I plan to marry her."

That didn't surprise Dare one little bit. What did surprise him was that Morton obviously hadn't asked Casey yet. What would she say when he did ask? Dare wondered. And how was he going to feel if Casey became another man's wife? The possibility didn't bear thinking about. "So, when's the big day?" he asked an instant after he'd told himself he wouldn't.

"Soon. Very soon."

"Then what I said before still goes." The look Dare gave Morton made him back up a step. "You treat her right."

"I plan to."

Dare wondered if Morton had the slightest notion how to handle Casey. She needed a firm hand, and he suspected Casey had Morton eating out of hers. How long would a man like Morton keep Casey happy? How happy had he already made her? That was something else Dare didn't want to think about.

"There's one thing you should know, Morton," he said with a growl.

"What's that?"

"Casey has no idea how sexy she looks in that bathing suit . . . or in anything else she wears, for that matter. If you make a big deal of it, you'll only embarrass her."

Miles shook his head, grinned, then chuckled. "I'm beginning to realize that Casey isn't the normal, run-of-the-mill lady. It plays havoc with a man's libido, doesn't it?"

"You've got that right," Dare agreed, laughing softly as he remembered how often Casey had done or said something to make him hard, and had been completely oblivious to his condition.

They were still laughing when Casey hurried back to the pool. Men, she thought, sighing in relief as she handed the file to Miles. She could never figure them out. But she wasn't about to ask them what was so funny.

Casey kept giving Dare anxious glances while Miles hung around, making desultory conversation. Finally, she was unable to restrain herself any longer. "Look, Miles, I'm really sorry, but I think you should leave. Dare's going to be exhausted before we even get started on his exercises."

"Yes, well . . . I was hoping to take you out to dinner tonight," Miles said.

"I . . . I don't know. I don't—" She cast another anxious glance at Dare.

Dare frowned, his eyes glinting with anger. "Remember our deal, Casey."

"Still—"

"Casey Amelia Boone, I'm warning ya."

Casey smiled down at Dare, not the least bit intimidated by his threatening tone of voice.

"I'd love to go out to dinner with you," she told Miles. "But not tonight. I want to make sure Dare is settled in before I leave him."

"Hmmph!"

"Tomorrow night, then," Miles said quickly.

"I'm not deliberately putting you off, Miles, but I have plans for tomorrow that I can't change. I'm sorry."

"What plans?" Dare grumbled from the pool.

Miles ignored him. "And I'll be tied up at a conference in Dallas all week. What about next Saturday? We'll have dinner, then go dancing."

"Ah . . ." She hesitated, waiting for Dare to object this time. Had he forgotten that Saturday was her birthday? When Dare glared at her, she sighed in disappointment. "Yes. Saturday's fine."

"Walk me to the car and we'll decide where to go," Miles requested, placing his hand on Casey's shoulder. "See you around, King."

"Yeah, sure," Dare muttered, his eyes warning the doctor to keep his hand on her shoulder.

Dammit all to hell, Dare thought as he watched them disappear. He didn't cotton to the idea of Morton dating Casey, or doing anything else with her either. Casey was—no, Casey *wasn't* his.

He swallowed hard, trying to rid his mouth of the bad taste that filled it every time he thought of Casey with Morton. The taste, however, was still present when Casey reappeared and slipped into the pool again.

"What the hell do you see in him, anyway?" he asked, his voice harsh.

Casey stared at Dare in surprise, then stepped back into deeper water as she saw the dangerous glint in his eyes. "We have many things in common."

"You both work at the same hospital. What else?"

"We both like riding, and ballroom dancing . . . and we don't want to have—" Children, she finished silently, unable to admit that to Dare. Besides, he wouldn't believe her. Especially when he had insisted, and she had agreed, that they have at least six.

The ballroom-dancing bit was a low blow, Dare thought. Casey knew how much he enjoyed dancing with her. Would he ever take her dancing again? "Have what? Sex?" he said through clenched teeth.

"King, that was rude and uncalled for. Your mother would wash your mouth out with soap if she heard you talking to me that way."

"Yeah. Well, Morton is all wrong for you. He's too soft. You'll lead him around by the nose like a prize bull."

"It might have escaped your notice, King, that I am a grown woman now. My love life is no concern of yours. So let's drop this discussion and get on with your exercises."

"I keep forgetting," he said softly, his eyes caressing her. "All I am to you now is a patient."

"That's right," she said, trying to ignore the havoc his beautiful brown eyes were creating in all her vital organs. The only way she could get through these next few weeks was to keep things on a professional basis. She'd treat him as if he were a patient—one of the children under her care.

"It doesn't matter that once we were lovers?"

"Once. That's the operative word, Dare," she blurted out. "We were lovers only once."

"A mistake I'm beginning to regret."

Casey stared at Dare, wishing the pool would open up and she could sink to China. She'd thought Dare had enjoyed making love to her, but obviously he hadn't. She turned away, not wanting him to see how much his words had hurt her.

Dare swore softly as he gazed at her rigid shoulders. It was just like Casey to believe that their lovemaking hadn't meant anything to him.

When, in fact, it had been the best thing that had ever happened to him. His only regret was he'd waited so long to make her his, and despite everything that had happened between them, he hadn't made an effort to keep her.

He should have come back to see Casey after he'd tamed the well that had killed Cas, but he'd deliberately stayed away. Over and over again he'd told himself that Casey would be better off without him messing up her life, causing her heartaches and concern. Told himself that he would be happy, as long as Casey was happy.

He'd lied.

Dammit all to hell, he resented the fact that Casey had another man in her life, resented the possibility that Morton might one day live on the Rocking R with Casey, have children with Casey. But he couldn't tell her that now. Not when he couldn't even move his toe.

He ground his molars together, struggling to control his feelings . . . feelings he'd never experienced before, and was ashamed to admit to having now. Jealousy, the green-eyed monster, had no right to raise its ugly head around Casey.

Finally he managed to control his feelings, but not his hand, which shook slightly as he touched her shoulder. "I'm sorry, Casey. Maybe we should call off the exercises."

She turned to face him, her chin raised stubbornly. "No, we'll do them. That's what you're here for, isn't it?"

The second she touched his arm she realized she was in trouble. The awareness, the intense feelings she had experienced that morning when she was working on him in bed returned—a hundredfold. The smooth leather of his skin was now silken with water. His tanned shoulders looked massive, and the thick mat of hair on his chest looked so sexy, enticing her to untangle the springy knots and make new ones.

Something smoldered in his eyes, making her bones melt and her knees feel so weak, she could barely stand. She averted her gaze, deliberately tightening her hold on his arm. "I want you to lie back in the water, Dare, and I'll pull you across the pool while you try to kick your legs."

He gave her a half smile. "I have a feeling this is going to be more dangerous than jumping my motorbike across Devil's Drop-off."

"You're lucky you didn't break your fool neck in that escapade." She shuddered, remembering how terrified she'd been when she'd learned what he was going to do. Dare had ignored her pleas not to make the jump. Even then, he didn't seem to care if he got killed . . . and left her. So she'd gone and watched in horror as he'd roared up to the edge of the canyon, then soared across.

"I know," Dare said. "You told me so afterward, in no uncertain terms. Then you didn't speak to me for days."

"And you're about to get the silent treatment again, if you don't do what you're told."

He stared at the water with trepidation. Despite the daredevil stunts he'd attempted—and pulled off—in his youth, the only time he'd almost died was when he'd miscalculated on his Houdini trick. If Duke hadn't hauled him out of the pool, he'd have drowned. He'd learned two valuable lessons that day—which he still lived by and drummed into his crew: always check and double-check your equipment and always have an escape route planned in case anything goes wrong.

There had been no way of escaping the anguish and guilt he'd felt when Cas had died. When Casey had left him. It would haunt his soul for the rest of his life.

Casey tugged impatiently on his arm. "Come on, Dare, move your butt."

"Yes, ma'am." He let go of the edge of the pool—and sank. Casey grabbed him, supporting him, her arms wrapped around his chest. His groping hands caught the edge of the pool, and he pulled himself toward it, trapping her body between his and the cement.

Her breasts swelled against his chest; her nipples hardened instantly. Deep inside she began to ache . . . with the need to love him once more. Could he feel her pulse throbbing? Could he hear her heart pounding? Did he know how much she wanted him?

His hot, hungry eyes gave her the answer.

"Look, Dare, maybe we'd better postpone this until tomorrow," she whispered, suddenly so breathless, she could barely speak. "You're already exhausted."

"Stop treating me like a child."

Lowering his head, he seared a kiss across her lips, shocking her, stealing the air out of her lungs. She gasped, opened her mouth, and he thrust his tongue inside, ravaging her in a sensuous, stimulating way. Desire flowed through her, simmering in her pores, burning hotter and hotter as he kept on kissing her. Her knees gave out, and she wrapped her arms around his neck, achingly aware that Dare had never kissed her this way before. His kisses had always been gentle, considerate . . . never raw, never hot, never demanding.

For the first time in her life, Dare was kissing her as if she were a woman. Kissing her hungrily, carnally, wantonly, making her totally aware of how much he wanted her . . . and how much she wanted him. She shouldn't want him, her mind cried out, she *must not* want him. Not if she was going to stay safe.

From somewhere, she summoned up the willpower to resist, but his kisses changed, became more gentle . . . no longer taking but giving instead. His giving sapped the last of her self-control, and when he started to pull away, she clung to his lips, begging him to stay. It had been such a long time since he'd held her in his arms, such a long time since he'd kissed her, and she didn't want him to leave. Not yet. Because, heaven help her, no matter how dangerous it was, she didn't want to stop kissing Dare.

He never wanted to stop kissing Casey, Dare thought, but he should. Right that very minute. Instead, he drew in a ragged breath and kissed her again, because it felt so good to be kissing Casey. It had been a hell of a long time since he'd kissed her, and he'd been so hungry for her. But that didn't excuse the way he'd forced himself on her, had branded her with his lips, had taken her with his tongue. He'd apologize, as soon as he'd had his fill.

Which might be never, he realized. Her lips were so generous, so giving; her body so pliant, so promising . . . so willing. It made him aware of how much he'd been missing, how much he *would be* missing if she married Morton.

Abruptly Dare tore his lips from hers, raised his head, and stared at her, his chest heaving as he sucked in a labored breath. Her lips were still parted, trembling; her eyes looked as stunned as he was feeling. He moved to the side, one arm braced against the edge of the pool for support, allowing her the freedom to move. Slowly she straightened away from him, slid her arms off his shoulders, and folded them under her heaving breasts.

"That should prove I'm not a child," Dare muttered, then drew in another breath. "And tell me, Casey? How do my kisses compare to the Third's?"

Without a word, Casey pulled herself out of the pool and fled.

FIVE

Dare had endured Casey's silence while she'd banged pots and pans in the kitchen the rest of the afternoon—knowing from past experience that it wasn't worth his life to try to talk to Casey when she was cooking. He had endured her silence during supper, because the chicken and dumplings and Many Berries cake she fed him was the best meal he'd tasted in ages, and he didn't want to spoil it. When he'd offered to do the dishes, she disappeared without saying a word. She still hadn't returned, and he couldn't go to bed with this silence between them.

He wheeled his chair out the kitchen door and along the path to the stables, hoping he would find her there. The sunbaked earth was slowly giving up its heat to the coming night, but it was already much cooler under the old oak trees. The night air was filled with the scent of roses, and he stopped the chair and breathed deeply.

His mother had planted the roses, wanting to give Casey's mother as much enjoyment as possible. Madre had also planted roses on the Regent Ranch, and Dare felt a sudden longing to go home. It was ironic. He had traveled the world, secure in the knowledge that when he was ready to give up the challenge of capping the next wild well, he could go home. Now he couldn't. Not when it meant making his mother cry.

He pushed the wheels again, raising dust the rest of the way down to the stables. The door stood open, and he bumped over the low sill into the cool interior. It smelled of hay, manure, and horseflesh, and once again he was assailed by a feeling of longing so intense, he could almost taste it.

Slowly he wheeled along the aisle, pausing to look at the red, Arabian horses in the stalls and pet an inquisitive nose, then two. Casey had always wanted horses; she was making one of her dreams come true. Would he ever share her dreams again?

She was in the end stall, brushing Sundancer, and the sight of her beautiful, red head leaning against the mare's flank made his heart ache.

More than everything else—his own horse, the ranch, even his family—he longed for Casey. Lord, how he missed her, he thought, giving the wheels another shove.

As he approached she turned to look at him, a soothing hand on Sundancer's arched neck.

"I figured I'd find you here," he said softly. "You always headed for the stable or the springs when you were upset, and I upset you. I'm sorry."

Upset was a mild word for what she was feeling, Casey thought as she began brushing Sundancer again. All Dare had to do was smile at her and her hormones began humming, and she'd been trying to ignore them for the past two weeks. She had her life all mapped out—a nice, safe, secure life that included her ranch, her horses, and her work with the children.

And then Dare had kissed her . . . and had blown all thoughts of safe, secure, and happy out of the water. Damn him anyway, she couldn't let him do that to her.

"I had no business kissing you like that," he continued when she remained silent. "Especially when I was angry and frustrated. I'll try to behave myself in the future."

She looked up, and he smiled at her, not his sexy smile but an endearing one, which could coax her to do anything—or almost anything. A grin flirted at the corners of her lips as she reluctantly responded to his charm. "So will I."

His smile faded. "I don't want you treating me like a child."

"I won't," she said, vowing she wouldn't make that mistake again. He was a very sexy, very potent, very dangerous man. "And I *didn't* today," she added for good measure as she ran the brush along Sundancer's back. "If I'd been treating you like a child, I wouldn't have left you alone in the pool."

"And I don't want your pity."

She shot him a surprised glance, then quickly looked away, wondering how on earth Dare could ever think she pitied him. "Pity is the last thing I feel when I think of you."

"So, will you give me another chance," he asked, gripping the rubber tires with his hands. If she wanted him to go, he would leave immediately. And if he were an honorable man, he wouldn't wait for her to tell him to leave. Morton was in her life now, and he should get the hell out of it.

"Tomorrow we'll start a new day," she said softly.

Relaxing his grip on the wheels, he flexed his aching fingers, then folded his arms across his chest. "Thanks, dar—" He cleared his husky throat and tried again. "Thanks, princess." They wouldn't start with a fresh slate—there were still too many things standing in the way—but at least he could be near Casey awhile longer.

Silently, she continued to brush the mare's glossy hide, and silently he watched her, thinking again how fortunate he'd been to find a colt the same color as her hair. She had such beautiful hair, so thick, and tumbled and sexy. He ached with the desire to weave his fingers through it, to bury his face in it, to see the flaming locks spread out on his pillow after they'd made love.

The images had an immediate effect on his body. He lowered his hands and began massaging his thigh, trying to hide the evidence of his desire. "Sundancer's looking good," he said, when he finally had things under control again. "Real good. And so are the stables. You've done a great job of fixing them up."

Casey smiled, pleased once again by his praise. But then Dare had always given her praise, she remembered suddenly. Something her father had rarely done. "It was a labor of love," she told Dare. "I know how much Dad always wanted to make Mama's dream of living in the big city come true, but I still remember how heartbroken I was when he sold the ranch so he could buy the condo in Houston."

"I remember too. It was only the second time in seventeen years that I'd ever seen you cry." He grinned, hiding a multitude of feelings. "But I also remember how you vowed that someday you'd come back here."

"It was also the night you promised we'd be buddies, no matter where I lived."

"That's right . . . I did," he said softly, also remembering his final words to her the last time they had met at the springs. *Maybe you should build a new life for yourself. Find another man. But I hope someday you'll be my buddy again.*

Casey had offered to be his friend again, and

his physical therapist, but not his buddy . . . his beloved buddy.

Giving Sundancer a final pat, Casey left the stall, secured the gate, then stepped over to hang the brush on the back wall. She turned and looked at Dare wistfully. "I guess Dad must have known how much I loved the ranch. The lawyer said he'd bought it back from the California dude so he could give it to me as a wedding present." She waved her hand at the horses. "But I would gladly give up the ranch if only Dad were alive."

Dare stared at her a moment, his eyes full of agony, then spun the chair around. Before he could move away, she stopped him by placing a hand on his shoulder. "Dare. I'm sorry."

"You're sorry! How do you think I feel?" he asked hoarsely, then drew in a ragged breath. "But nothing I can say or do will bring your father back to you."

"No, nothing can change what happened to Dad." Sliding her arms over his shoulders, she pressed her hands against his chest, unconsciously trying, she realized, to keep him safe. "But you could prevent the same thing from happening to yourself, Dare. You could stop fighting those fires. Now. Before they kill you too."

"Casey!"

Releasing him, she drew back slightly. "I'm sorry. I promised myself that I wouldn't nag you."

"Well, you might get your wish," Dare said, managing a lopsided smile.

"Never, in a million years, do I want you to quit because you *have* to. I want you to do it because you *want* to." She hugged him again, thinking that life had a way of playing horrible tricks on a person. More than anything, she wanted Dare safe, and here she was trying to help him walk again. When walking meant he'd return to his dangerous job. "Well, that's a decision you can make when you're on your feet again. And that's the last time I'm going to mention it. I promise." Giving him another hug, she straightened, but her fingers lingered on his shoulders, noting how tense they were.

He patted her hand and looked at her. This time his smile reached his eyes. "Thanks, princess."

They continued to gaze into each other's eyes, sharing a few more if-only-things-were-different moments, then Dare released Casey's hand, and she stepped back.

Dare pushed the wheels a couple of slow turns down the aisle and stopped. "I see you've bought some more horses," he said, indicating the stalls.

"Yeah, I've been splurging." He chuckled, and Casey grinned as she patted Sunshine's nose. "You know how much I love them."

"Almost as much as you love children." He felt another pang of guilt as he noticed the wary expression that suddenly clouded her face. "Morton is right, Casey. You should be working at the hospital, not spending your time looking after me."

She moved back to his side. "Don't worry. They'll manage fine without me."

"But the kids love you. Every time you walked into the courtyard, they latched onto you, even though some of them could barely move."

"They're special, aren't they. So brave. I wish I could do more for them."

He gazed at her in admiration, not in the least surprised by her words. "You're already giving them everything you've got . . . your expertise, your patience, your courage, laughter, and love. What more can you do?"

"I don't know. Something . . . special." Giving him a wry smile, she tapped her forehead. "The idea's floating around in there, somewhere, but I can't put my finger on it."

"Well, knowing you, you'll figure it out one of these days." Slowly he began wheeling the chair down the aisle, with Casey at his side. "And once you've figured out what it is, you'll do it, come hell or high water. You're one very stubborn lady."

"I had a great teacher."

"Don't blame your stubbornness on me. You were born with it."

"Here you've always told me I was the sweetest thing in the world."

"That too." Laughing softly, he waited for her to close the stable door, then they moved along the path toward the hacienda. "But seriously, Casey, I want you to go back to work. You can put me through my paces in the morning, and I'll keep at it for the rest of the day. Then, if you're not too tired, you can give me another workout at night when you get home."

"But—"

"No arguments, Casey. I'm feeling guilty enough as it is, imposing on you this way."

"We'll see." She opened the kitchen door and stood back to let him pass, then stepped in, flicked on the light, and closed the door. "Maybe I could work part-time. Some of the kids seem to respond better to me, and I don't want to set their program back too far."

"Good. Now that that's settled, I'll hit the sack."

She gazed down into Dare's eyes, wanting to prolong the evening, which, despite its rocky moments, had been one of the best she'd spent in years. Because she had spent it with Dare, she admitted. "Do you want something before you go to bed? A drink? Something to eat?"

Only you, he thought, quickly glancing away, hoping she hadn't read his mind. Once he had dreamed of sharing his evenings there on the ranch with Casey. Of bedding down the horses, then listening to Casey telling stories to their children as they bedded them down. Afterward, he'd sit by the fire, with Casey on his knee, and she'd tell him his own special story in her deep, warm, wonderful voice. And then he'd take her to bed and tell her a story the only way he knew how—with his lips, and his hands, and his body.

"Thanks," he said, his voice husky with dreams, "but I'm still full from supper."

"What about a back rub? Your shoulders are really tight."

"I'm fine, Casey."

"Then at least take a pain pill. You haven't had anything for days, and I know you're hurting."

"No, Casey, no more painkillers."

"But, Dare, it's foolish to be suffering so much."

He gave her a soft smile and warning shake of his head. "Stop fussing, princess. I honestly, truly don't need anything else." Except you . . . and to sleep without dreaming.

The dream came again, as it had so many nights during the last three years. The earth rumbled and shook in anger, the fire roared forth into the sky. And in the middle of the flames Cas stood, with his hand outstretched, imploring Dare for help.

Dare struggled to reach Cas, but he couldn't move. *He couldn't move.*

Cursing in frustration, he frantically tried to force one foot in front of the other. But something was holding him back. A ton of tar was lying on his legs.

He couldn't move and his best friend was dying before his eyes.

He cried out in anguish, the sound catching in the back of his throat.

"Dare, Dare, wake up." The soft voice became insistent. "Wake up, Dare. You're having a nightmare. It's all right. You're safe."

Still groaning, he reluctantly turned away from the fiery horror, leaving Cas . . . leaving his best friend. Opening his eyes, he saw the shadowy figure of Casey bending over him. With a trembling hand, he reached out and touched her arm. And discovered she was real, not the vision that had also haunted his dreams.

"It's your fault. Why didn't you make him stop?"

He'd never forget those words—and the others—she'd said that day. They were branded into his soul.

Casey reached out and brushed Dare's hair off his hot, damp forehead. "Dare, are you awake?"

He worked up enough spit to manage a harsh, "Yeah."

"You were having a bad dream."

An understatement, but he'd let it lie. "Yeah."

"Do you want to tell me about it?"

"No." Not if it meant causing her any more pain. He only hoped Casey didn't dream these hellish nightmares.

"Sometimes it helps to talk about it."

"Nothing will help."

She wanted to argue with him, to force him to tell her, but she wasn't ready to hear the words she knew he would say. Reaching over, she turned on the bedside light, hoping to banish the nightmare from both of their minds.

Dare blinked as the lamplight hit his eyes, then blinked again as he saw Casey. She was leaning over him, her hair flaming around her bare shoulders—wearing only a scrap of peacock-blue satin and lace that barely covered her curves.

"What the hell are you wearing?"

She straightened, instantly aware of how *little* she was wearing. "A teddy."

"Do you wear it for him?"

"Who?"

"The Third. Your lover."

"Miles is *not* my lover. How double-dare you say such a thing!" She pressed her hands to her bosom—and became even more aware of the cleavage showing between the two strips of lace that masqueraded as a camisole. Picking up Dare's shirt from the chair, she slipped into it and quickly buttoned it from top to bottom. It billowed around her and didn't cover much of her legs, but at least she was decent again.

"I—I bought this teddy and six more like it for our honeymoon," she stammered, barely able to meet his eyes. "They've been buried in my dresser —the one you're now using—until yesterday."

His eyes grew darker, his gaze more intimate. "So, why are wearing one now, after all these years?"

Heaven only knew why she had decided to wear one, because the excuse she'd given herself as she'd slipped into it—the one about having to wear *something* to bed because she now had a man in the house—no longer held water when Dare was looking at her with such an unholy gleam in his eyes.

"I . . . I decided I didn't want them to go out of fashion."

A smile tugged at the corner of his lips. "Oh, Casey, Casey. There's no danger of that happening." He chuckled softly. "And I kinda like what you do for my shirt too."

"Don't you double-dare laugh at me." She giggled as she remembered the story she'd been wanting to share with Dare for years. "I'll have you know I went to great lengths, suffered untold embarrassment, to buy these pieces of fluff for you."

"Tell me," Dare coaxed, giving her his wide, beguiling smile as he bunched the sheet over his middle and patted the mattress.

She stared at him, hesitating for a moment. Then because, after all, he was Dare, the buddy she used to tell everything to, she sat down on the bed, curled her feet up under her, and pulled his shirt down over her legs.

"Well, I slunk into one of those little shops," she said, putting on her best storytelling voice. "You know, the kind with curtains on the windows so no one can see who's inside. And the saleslady takes one look at me and almost shows me the door. I guess she didn't think I belonged in there. And I didn't! You should see all the . . . the *things* they have in . . ."

Dare lay there, watching her animated face and listening to the sound of her bluesy, honey-on-bourbon voice. Afraid that if he listened to her words, he'd become so aroused, he'd do something unforgivable—like haul her down beside him and strip his shirt and that tempting teddy off her body. The sight of her beautiful breasts, barely covered by those scraps of cloth, had made him thankful he was covered by a sheet. It didn't help matters that her hair was glowing like a torch, and her skin was so warm, he could feel the heat, and she smelled of morning dew and wildflowers. Everything about Casey made him want to curl up beside her and spend the rest of his days listening to her stories.

To think his buddy had once wanted to please him . . . had gone shopping for lingerie to wear for him . . .

". . . and I almost strangled myself on one of those bras," Casey said, rolling her eyes and fanning her face with her hand. "You know the kind with all those straps and the red feathers and the holes in the, ahem . . . strategic places."

He choked back the laughter as he pictured the scene of his tomboy Casey trying to figure out what went where.

"I wanted to holler for help, but I didn't want to admit to the sexy saleslady that I didn't know the first thing about erotic lingerie. So I kept tying myself in knots . . . trying to make it . . .

ahem . . . cover my breasts. And then I realized I was trying to put on the panties—not the bra."

Dare hooted, then thumped the mattress and howled with laughter. He tried to stop but couldn't. It had been such a long time since he'd felt like laughing, and Casey's story had broken the dam. He laughed until he was breathless, the tears rolled down his cheeks, and his stomach ached. And as he laughed hope slipped silently back into his heart.

Casey laughed, too, rocking back and forth with her mirth. But even as she laughed she watched and listened to Dare. His laughter was rusty from disuse, she realized, and wished she'd trotted out a funny story days ago. Wished, also, that she'd had enough courage to tell him stories and make him laugh these past three years. It was the least she could do for the bighearted man who had done so much for her.

Her laughter died, and when his died, too, she finished the story, still watching him. "When I finally managed to escape from the elastic-and-feather trap, I decided I'd better stick to something that had all the holes in the right places and asked to see their teddies. By that time I was as red as a tomato, so when the lady showed me the choices in my size, I bought everything on the rack and ran."

He laughed again, more softly this time, and reached out to take her hand, pressing it to his lips. "Thanks, Casey. I needed that."

For long moments they gazed at each other,

both achingly aware of other things they needed. Slowly Casey withdrew her hand, then pushed herself off the bed. "You need more," she said huskily. "Roll over. I'm going to give you that massage I should have given you before you went to bed. Your muscles are as tight as a drum; it's no wonder you're hurting."

"I'm not hurting," he said automatically, although his back and legs were throbbing. That pain was lightweight, however, compared with the heavy-duty way his heart ached because he'd lost his beautiful, wonderful, funny Casey.

"King, I'm getting tired of your macho act. Now roll over and let me see what color shorts you're wearing."

"Purple with red hearts," he muttered as he did as he was told. Raising his head, he looked at her over the curve of his arm and asked suspiciously, "You didn't, by chance, buy them for me?"

"Well, someone had to. But let me tell you, I was redder than a beet by the time I got out of that store. Do you know how many styles of men's briefs you can buy?" She flushed again as she remembered the incredulous look on the clerk's face when she'd blurted out that they had to fit a giant.

"Until two weeks ago I wore plain, white cotton—as you well know." He shot her a wicked grin. "But thanks to you, I'm learning, real quick."

She wiggled her nose at him as she bent over to pull back the sheet. The oversized shirt fell away from her body. Dare took one look at what the gaping neckline revealed and buried his head in the pillow.

"Oh, Lord," he said with a groan.

"What's the matter?" Casey asked in concern as she went to work on him, her fingers flying up and down his spine, hitting all the sore spots gently at first, then with enough pressure to relieve the tension.

"Ah . . . nothing, sweet Casey. Ah, that feels so good . . . Yes. There. That's the spot. And there." And because he knew there was nothing sexual about the way Casey was touching him, he managed—just barely—to keep his body under control, to remember that he was just a patient to Casey, not a man she had once known.

Casey continued to massage Dare, wishing there were some way she could work the pain out of his body, wishing she could heal him with the magic of her touch, wishing they'd wake up and discover that the last three years had been a bad dream.

Gradually the awareness she'd been holding at bay finally surfaced—awareness of Dare as a man, not a patient, of his broad, powerful shoulders, of the strength and beauty of his long back, of the warmth of his skin and the scent of sandalwood and spice. All the things she shouldn't be noticing, she warned herself sternly . . . if she were going to get through the next few months with her plans still intact.

With a final soft rub, she lifted her hands from

his shoulders. He raised his head and gazed at her, his eyes not quite as sleepy as she would have wished.

"Thanks, Casey, that was great," he said as he turned onto his back, thankful, too, that there was no erection to embarrass her.

"Anytime." She leaned over to fluff up his pillow, then straightened slightly, gazing down at him in concern. "Will you be able to sleep now?"

"Yes, princess."

"You're lying, Dare."

Raising his big hand, he brushed his knuckles along her jaw. "I could never fool you, could I?"

His gentle touch sent a shiver of delight down her spine, and it was a moment before she could whisper huskily, "What can I do to help?"

He started to smile, then thought better of it. "You . . . could lie down beside me," he said, lowering his hand to the bed.

Suddenly she became aware of his vast expanse of naked flesh, and the fact that she was wearing only his shirt over a skimpy teddy. But Dare had always behaved like a gentleman toward her, had always treated her as if she were a princess—except today in the pool. "Dare . . . I don't think that would be a good idea."

"I'm not suggesting we . . . make love. I . . ." He gazed at her earnestly, hoping she would trust him. "I just want to hold you the way I used to a long time ago."

"And that would put you to sleep?"

"It worked every time . . . but I'll understand if you don't want to take the risk, if you can't—"

"Shush," she said, knowing she could trust him despite the kiss. "You know I can never refuse you when you smile at me."

"I didn't smile," he said huskily, watching her with innocent brown eyes.

"I know. That's why I'm going to get into bed with you. On top of the sheet." Quickly, before she could change her mind, she pulled the sheet up to cover his chest, turned out the light, then lay down beside him. "I don't remember ever doing this," she said into the darkness, very aware of his big, warm body only inches away from hers.

"You were just a baby."

"So, what do I do now?"

"Put your head on my shoulder and snuggle close."

Slowly she did as she was told, but she lay tense in his arms.

He laughed softly. "I don't blame you for being suspicious, princess, but all I want to do is touch you like this."

Raising his hand, he laid it against her head, then began gently stroking the sensitive skin below Casey's ear with the side of his forefinger. That's all he did, just moved his finger lazily back and forth, back and forth, as his breathing slowed and deepened.

After the first moment of surprise, Casey relaxed, feeling reassured by his touch. It was a familiar sensation, but she couldn't remember Dare ever touching her this way before, even though his marvelous hands had explored every inch of her body, had known her intimately.

Why, then, did she feel so safe, so loved, so cherished because Dare was stroking her cheek?

The question flirted through her mind as she lay contentedly in his arms. Gradually his finger slowed, then stopped, and she knew that Dare finally slept. She wondered if she should move, then decided against it; she didn't want to risk waking him up again. Perhaps she, too, would sleep.

Sleep, however, did not come. Instead, she lay there in the strong arms of the man she had once planned to marry, listening to his heart beat . . . and grieving over the loss of his love.

It was her fault they hadn't married, her fault she had no legal right to lay her head on the pillow next to his. But even if she could turn back the clock and live their wedding day over again, she still couldn't walk down the aisle to him. Not if she had to live with the constant fear that someday he would walk out the door and not return. Not when she also lived with the fear that one day the time bomb inside her head would explode.

SIX

Dare woke refreshed, more rested, more relaxed than he'd felt since he'd been injured . . . longer than that if the truth were known.

And the reason he was feeling so good was because Casey was lying in his arms—where she belonged. Sometime during the night he had thrown off the sheet and now her cheek was resting on his chest above his heart. His fingers were burrowed in her hair, holding her tightly as if he'd known, even in his sleep, that he never wanted to let her go.

But he had no right to hold Casey. No right at all. The previous night had been a gift from the gods to show him a glimpse of heaven.

Today he would descend once more into hell.

He gripped her head tighter, and his arm pressed her body closer to his chest. She woke, tried to raise her head, and when he relaxed his grip, gazed at him in confusion.

"Dare?" She smiled as she recognized the man who was holding her, then frowned as she saw the dark misery in his beautiful brown eyes. "What's the matter?"

"Please, C-Casey." His voice cracked, and he swallowed hard. "Please say you forgive me."

"Forgive you? Whatever for?"

"I'll never forget what you told me on our wedding day," he said hoarsely, knowing he had to get it out in the open regardless of what it would cost him. "You said: *It's your fault Dad is dead. Your fault there isn't enough of his body left to bury.*"

Casey stared at Dare in stunned silence. What had she done to the man she once loved? The evidence was written starkly on Dare's face, making her heart ache. "Oh, Dare." She touched his arm, but he brushed her hand away. "Did I say that to you?" she whispered.

With a groan, he threw his arm up to cover his face. He couldn't bear to look at her any longer, couldn't bear to see the condemnation in her eyes. "Among other things," he said, his voice muffled.

"I'm so sorry." She touched his arm again, then gripped it firmly, needing both hands to circle its muscular girth. "I was upset that day, numb with shock. I didn't realize I'd said those horrible things to you."

"I deserved every word, and more."

"No, Dare. I shouldn't have blamed you for

Dad's death." She pulled at his arm, trying to lift it away from his face. "Please, Dare, look at me."

Slowly he let his arm flop to the side and looked at her, his cheeks wet with tears. "But you were right," he cried out, his throat so tight, he could barely speak. "It was my fault Cas died. He was sixty-eight. Too old to be fighting fires. I should have found a way to make him quit."

"Hush," Casey whispered, leaning over to kiss away a tear.

"He . . . he was my best friend. The man I loved as much as my brothers . . . my father." His voice broke again. "And because of me, he's dead."

"Hush, Dare, hush. It wasn't your fault." Cupping his face between her hands, she tenderly tried to stem his tears, kissing them away with her lips, brushing them away with her fingers. They kept on flowing. "I'm so sorry I blamed you, Dare. I know how much you loved him."

Resting her cheek against his, she let her own tears flow, tears of sorrow for Dare, for *his* loss. She had cried the day of her father's death, she remembered, but Dare hadn't. He had just stood there and held her, had bottled up his grief so he could be strong for her. Now it was her turn to hold him.

She snuggled closer, pressing her arms against his sides, holding him tight. His arm came up and cradled her, his hand tangled in her hair, and they held each other and cried.

Lord, how he loved Casey, Dare thought as he cuddled her body closer. He had loved her all his life, but never more than he did now, when she was holding him, crying with him. He shouldn't be crying. He should have remained strong for her. And he would be strong again, soon, but right now all he wanted to do was hold her. To let the knowledge sink into his brain; Casey didn't blame him for her father's death.

For the last three years Dare had lived with the pain, the guilt, the grief of Cas's death, and so his tears continued to flow . . . until gradually the nightmares receded from his mind, the black demons disappeared from his soul, and peace returned to his heart.

"I'm sorry," he whispered eventually into her tear-dampened hair.

Raising her head, she smiled down at him, her green eyes full of tears. "Don't you dare, double-dare, say another word about being sorry," she warned, then reached over and snatched some tissues out of the box on the bedside table. After handing him one, she blew her nose on another and mopped up her eyes. He did the same, watching her sheepishly. Finished, she dropped a kiss on his lips, then snuggled back into his arms, shifting her hip to rest against his side and settling her leg over his.

Dare held her with one arm, his fingers soothing her hair. "I tried . . ."

"Tried what? Please talk to me, Dare. Tell me

how you feel. Don't keep things bottled up any longer."

He drew in a ragged breath. "I tried talking to Cas," he said hoarsely, then cleared his raw throat. "Hundreds of times, but I couldn't make myself say the words. He was so proud. So stubborn. It would have hurt him badly if I'd told him he was slowing up, that he had to quit. Can you understand that, Casey?"

"Yes," she said, gently rubbing his shoulder. Although she hadn't known her father well, she could understand how he felt because he and Dare were cut from the same cord of wood—and she knew Dare. Pride was Dare's middle name. What was going to happen to him if he couldn't walk again? Couldn't fight fires again?

"Cas always told me that if he couldn't fight fires, he was no longer a man," Dare said quietly. "It was his life."

"I know," Casey said sadly. "He loved fighting fires more than he loved my mother."

"He loved your mother, Casey. He might not have had the courage to come home each night, but he did love her."

She moved her head against Dare's chest. "Maybe he did love her, but he hated me. If it weren't for me—for my being born—mother wouldn't have been sick."

"Casey!" Dare gave her a quick, reassuring hug. "Casey, darlin', that's not true. He loved you." He hugged her again, then gently brushed his fingers through her hair. "Not a day went by that Cas didn't tell me how much he loved you, what a smart kid you were. How proud he was of you. Ask any of the boys and they'll tell you the same thing."

"Then why didn't he come home?" she cried out, allowing the hurt she'd always hidden finally to burst forth. "Why wasn't he there for my birthdays? For Christmas? For my graduation? And don't tell me it was because he had to work. You were also fighting the same fires, but you managed to be home for most Christmases. You made it to my graduation. And if you couldn't be home for my birthdays, at least you remembered to send a present. Why couldn't my own father do the same thing? He had time to run off to Vegas and Reno. Why couldn't he come home to Mother and me?"

"I don't know what drove the man, Casey," Dare said as he continued to stroke her hair. "Except . . . I think he felt he was a failure. Cas wanted lots of children, and blamed himself when they didn't have any. He once told me he thought a miracle had happened when he learned Elise was pregnant with you. Your mother was forty by that time and was afraid she was too old to have a child. Then she had the stroke while she was in labor, and Cas felt guilty for insisting they keep trying. He also felt guilty for not providing her with the city life he'd promised when they were married. So he kept on working his butt off, and when there wasn't any work, he hid his guilt and sorrow by raising hell."

Guilt, she thought as Dare's words finally helped her understand her parents and herself. It hadn't taken her long to figure out that her parents didn't have a normal relationship, and who was really to blame. She'd done her best to make it up to her mother, but every time she'd seen her mother's frustration, because she couldn't speak and could barely move, Casey had felt guilty. And the guilt had doubled in magnitude on the few occasions her father had come home.

That was why she'd desperately wanted Cas to walk her down the aisle. If he showed up, she had reasoned, it would mean he finally had forgiven her. That was why his ultimate desertion had been so devastating; she hadn't had a chance to be forgiven.

"He was going to quit," Dare said softly, wondering even as he spoke whether his words were going to hurt Casey or help her finally lay her father to rest. "He told me when we got engaged that he was going to stop fighting fires as a wedding gift to you. Then right before the wedding that well blew in West Texas. I was mopping up the one in Algeria, so he decided he'd kill it. He did it for us, princess. He didn't want us to have to postpone our honeymoon." Cas also had other reasons for wanting to kill the well. Reasons Dare had discovered an hour before the wedding. They'd smashed all his dreams into the dust, but he still hoped and prayed that Casey would never learn what her father had done.

"Oh, Dare." Casey sighed, her breath warming his skin. "There's so much. . . ."

"I know," he said, absently running his hand up and down her back. There was so much between them, so many memories. He prayed that someday Casey would remember only the happy times and not the sad. Lord knew, she'd had a hard life, but she'd never complained, had always taken what fate had dished up with a smile on her lips and joy in her heart.

That was why he loved her so dearly.

Abruptly he became aware that she was nestled trustingly against him . . . too trustingly. He could feel the softness of her breasts against his chest, the velvet of her thigh as it lay intimately between his. Somehow his hand had worked its way beneath the shirt she wore and was resting against her bare back. Her skin was smoother than the satin of her teddy. He brushed a finger between the teddy and her skin, relishing the differences.

He could make love to Casey, Dare thought. She was so relaxed and willing that all he had to do was turn her over and make her his.

But she was also vulnerable, physically as well as emotionally. If she and Morton weren't lovers, he doubted she was taking the pill, and he had no way of protecting her.

He ground his teeth, barely keeping back an oath of frustration.

"What's the matter?" she murmured.

He laughed harshly, realizing Casey still didn't know the potent effect she had on him. Deliberately he pulled her up against his pelvis.

She snuggled closer, then froze. He was hard and hot and throbbing against her, separated by only two thin layers of cloth. "Oh, dear!"

"That's what's the matter, Casey." His big, warm hand caressed her bottom, urging her closer.

Honeyed heat washed through her, pooling between her thighs. She held herself rigid, fighting the temptation to relax against Dare and let nature take its course. "Oh, dear."

"We've spent an interesting five hours in this bed, darlin'," he drawled as he reluctantly raised his hand. "We've laughed together, we've cried. And if you don't move in the next ten seconds, we're going to be making love."

"Oh, dear." Gathering herself together, she slid out of bed. On trembling legs, which threatened to collapse, she fled. His soft laughter followed her.

Why had she fled? Casey asked herself for the hundredth time as she rattled the lid on the bean pot, then banged a few more pans for good measure, hoping the noise would make Dare stay in the living room. She didn't want him anywhere near the kitchen. It would spoil her surprise. Besides, it was too difficult to think when he was around, too hard to sort out her emotions.

She had fled, she admitted, because she was afraid. In the space of a few hours she'd been through an emotional wringer with Dare, experiencing anger, regret, and sorrow, but also feeling happier, more content than she'd felt in years. However, she still didn't know how she really felt about Dare.

Nor how he felt about her. In fact he'd *never* told her how he felt about her. She didn't even know why he'd asked her to marry him.

"Casey!" Dare called from the next room. "What the devil's going on? The family's car is coming up the drive!"

Wiping her hands on the dish towel, she dashed into the living room and stopped short at the sight of Dare sitting in his wheelchair in the middle of the room. He looked so breathtakingly sexy in the chino shirt he'd pulled on after their session in the pool. He hadn't bothered to do up the laces, and his chest hair filled the opening of his shirt, creating havoc with her nerves. And the way his tan jeans stretched across his thighs, hugging him like a second skin, made her heart-thumpingly aware of his masculinity. He'd been in her house less than forty-eight hours and already she was a basket case! She would never survive if she didn't get her feelings under control—and fast.

"What are they doing here?" he asked, glaring up at her.

She took a deep breath, pressed her hands against her racing heart. "They want to make sure that you're all right. They were all set to storm the hospital, so I promised I'd invite them over as soon as you got out."

"So that's what you've been up to." He laughed softly, shaking his head. "I should have known. Well, let's get the show on the road."

She watched as he squared his shoulders and lifted his head proudly, and felt herself relax for the first time since she'd begun planning this meeting. Dare would survive; she only hoped the others wouldn't react badly to the sight of him in the wheelchair. "King, that pride of yours is going to be the death of you yet," she muttered in admiration as she walked to the door. Opening it wide, she called out, "Hello, everyone. Come on in."

Dare watched his family enter the room, a forced smile on his lips. A moment later his mother was in his arms, kissing him, and everything was all right.

"Hello, darling, it's so good to see you," Madre King said, lifting her head to look at him, her lips trembling, her face full of love.

Dare patted her cheek. "It's good to see you, too, Madre, but don't you dare start crying all over me."

"No, Darrick, I won't. You're alive, you're home. And I thank God for His blessings."

She rested her forehead against Dare's, and he held her, patting her shoulder, loving the woman who had always understood his need to live on the edge, to test the fates. "I'm sorry for worrying you, Madre," he whispered. "I don't know how you put up with me."

"Well, this time Casey's been nominated." Releasing Dare, Madre walked to Casey's side and gave her a hug. "It's a good thing we have you in the family, my dear. I don't know what we'd do without you."

Dare gazed at the two women he loved most in the world. His mother, slim and elegant in a pink suit, and Casey, looking very feminine in white jeans and a multicolored shirt with long, white, sheer sleeves.

Then the third lady he loved, his grandmother, leaned over, kissed his cheek, and offered her soft cheek for his kiss. "It's good to have you home again, boy. I hope you'll stop running around the country now and settle down."

"I'll give it some thought," Dare said, smiling at her. His smile faded as his father entered the room, leaning heavily on the cane he'd used since his stroke.

The Baron took one look at Dare then turned away, his face drawn, his lips tight. Without a word he limped over to the big stone fireplace, deliberately turned a chair away from Dare, and sat down.

Suddenly Casey was at Dare's side, her hand on

his shoulder. He glanced up, saw the concern on her face, and gave her a reassuring wink.

"You're looking very elegant today, Duchess," Dare said to his grandmother, who was regal in royal blue. "What's the occasion?"

"We've been to the chapel to christen David King, the Eighth," Duke, the oldest King brother, answered for his grandmother as he walked into the room, one arm around his wife, Marnie, the other holding a baby dressed in white christening robes.

"Duke, you old son of a gun! Congratulations." Dare grinned at his brother in delight. "A boy. When was he born?"

The tall, black-haired president of King Oil gazed at his infant son, his aristocratic features tender with love. "Ten days ago. Thank goodness Marnie managed to hang on until I got home from Colombia, or I would have been in deep trouble."

"I wanted to tell you, Dare, but Marnie insisted on giving you the news herself," Casey said softly, watching as the beautiful, redheaded woman took the sleeping baby from Duke and carefully placed him in Dare's arms. Marnie gazed at Dare with so much adoration in her eyes, Casey would have been jealous—if Dare was hers—and if she hadn't seen the besotted way Marnie looked at her husband.

Dare cuddled the baby in one arm and hugged Marnie with the other. "Marnie, honey. I'm so happy for you."

"Thanks, Dare, for . . . for all your gifts," Marnie whispered as she kissed him. She straightened, and for a moment she looked as if she were going to cry. Then she managed a smile as she hugged him again. "How do you feel about being an uncle?"

"Proud as the dickens," Dare said, gazing down at his black-headed nephew then back at Marnie, thinking that fortune had definitely smiled on Duke the day Marnie had sailed into his life.

"I thought that feeling was reserved for the brand-new father," Duke said as he lifted his son back into his arms. Bending his head, he kissed the baby's cheek, then smiled at Marnie. Together they moved to the brown leather couch and sat down, totally absorbed in each other and their baby.

Casey watched, marveling at the difference Marnie had made in Duke's life. His first marriage and divorce had turned the man she loved like a brother into a cold, hard, remote man. Now he laughed and sang again, and it was all thanks to Marnie. Duke had married his "seawitch" aboard their boat, the *Believing Heart*, then had sailed with her through the Panama Canal on their honeymoon. The fact that he had never once flown home to look after business proved to Casey how much Duke loved Marnie.

"The grandmother is proud as punch too," Madre said as she sat down on the matching love seat and beamed at the baby.

The Duchess sat down beside her and smoothed her skirt over her knees. "Not to mention the great-grandmother."

"You've done us all proud, Marnie my love," Duke said as he bent his head to give her a kiss.

He looked so happy, Dare thought, watching his brother. And he deserved it; he'd been unhappy for such a long time. Thank God for Marnie, and thank God, too, for the baby Duke had once believed he'd never have.

Dare glanced up at Casey and saw that she was watching the baby, her lips parted softly, her eyes bright with longing. How many times had he dreamed of holding her baby in his arms? Dare wondered sadly. Too many to count. If they'd gotten married three years earlier, their baby would be walking and talking by now. Perhaps they'd have another one on the way. But giving Casey babies was no longer in his cards. Especially when she was thinking of marrying Morton.

The sound of another vehicle arriving in the yard intruded into Dare's thoughts. The front door opened again and Dev, the charismatic, crusading congressman, and his wife, Kristi, entered the living room, arms around each other, laughing at a private joke.

"Dev! Kristi! I didn't know you were here," Dare said. "I thought you'd be back in Washington."

"We couldn't miss the christening," Dev, the

youngest of the King brothers, explained. "Had to see how it's done."

"And we couldn't miss seeing you, either," Kristi said, bending over to give Dare a hug. "I wanted to thank you in person for the lovely wedding gift you sent us."

"You like it?" Dare asked, remembering his pleasure when he'd found a tapestry wall hanging of geese flying across the setting sun. It seemed as if it had been made specially for Kristi, who had a special kind of love for birds, and for Dev.

"Like it? She loves it," Dev said. "Thank goodness you have good taste, big brother, because Kristi insisted on hanging it in our living room. It takes up the whole wall."

Standing on tiptoes, Kristi brushed a kiss on Dev's cheek. "Don't give him a hard time, Dev. You know you love it too."

Dev placed his arm around Kristi and dropped a kiss into her white-blond hair.

"You two look as if you're still on your honeymoon," Dare said, thinking that Dev, too, had been very fortunate to find a woman like Kristi to stand beside him. Kristi was a true-blue crusader.

"Give us time to come down from the clouds," Dev said, laughing. "We've only been married since Valentine's day."

"I suspect you'll always glow when you're around Kristi," Dare teased.

"Yeah, there's a way a man looks at a woman when he's in love." Dev shot a knowing glance at

Duke, who was busy looking at his wife in that very special way. "Or so I've been told."

"And there's a way a woman looks when she's pregnant," the Duchess said, beaming at Kristi. "When's the happy occasion, my dear?"

"He's going to be a Christmas baby," Dev said proudly.

"*She*," Kristi said, unashamedly hugging Dev.

"Oh, how absolutely wonderful!" Marnie smiled up at them, making it very obvious what she thought of motherhood. "Why didn't you tell us?"

"We weren't going to say anything until after we finished celebrating David's birth," Kristi explained softly.

The Duchess clapped her hands. "That's what I like, lots of young'uns. It's about time you boys got busy. Now, all we have to do is get Dare married off."

"It was a good thing, Casey, that you didn't marry Dare," the Baron said, breaking his brooding silence as he rose to his feet. "You would have been stuck with a cripple for the rest of your life."

"Baron!" his wife admonished, rising to go to his side.

Casey wheeled to face them, hands on her hips, her body sheltering Dare from his father's angry eyes. "I have forbidden Dare to use that word, Baron, and I won't have you using it either."

He glared at her. "A spade is a spade, and it's black."

"And so is a club, but I am not going to let you bury Dare or beat him over the head, either."

Dare laughed, shaking his head.

"Casey's at it again," Duke said to Marnie. "Protecting Dare. We never could lift a hand against him without Casey flying to his rescue."

"Didn't I tell you Casey was as protective toward Dare as you are toward those birds of yours," Dev told Kristi.

Casey frowned at Dare in disbelief. "I don't do that, do I?"

"Yes you do," Dare said as he reached out to take her hand. "You always have."

For long moments they gazed at each other, Dare smiling as he remembered all the times little Casey had "mothered" him and how much he'd enjoyed it. Dare raised Casey's hand, pressed a kiss against her palm, then lowered it again, still holding it as he continued to smile at her.

Casey returned his smile, feeling so touched by his gesture, she didn't know whether to laugh or cry. And remembering, too, how Dare had never, ever, laughed at her or put her down when she'd been trying to "look after" him.

Dev watched them, a thoughtful expression on his face, then looked over at Marnie and finally down at his wife. "Ah, Kristi, honey. Let's go and unload Dare's horse."

"Rebel?" Dare tore his eyes away from Casey's to give his brother a surprised look. "You brought him here?"

"He's been kicking up such a fuss the last few weeks that no one wants to look after him, so I thought we'd bring him over," Madre put in quickly. "It will give you something to do in your free time."

"Free time. What's that? Casey's a real slave driver." Dare smiled at Casey again, making sure she knew how grateful he was for all her help. Casey smiled back, pleased that Dare was now feeling comfortable enough about accepting her help that he could tease her about it.

Laughing softly, Dev gave Kristi a quick hug. "And as soon as we unload Rebel, I think we'll borrow the car and run into town. Dare looks as if he might need some . . . ah, reading material."

"There are lots of books in the study," Casey said, giving Dev a puzzled glance.

"Yeah, well. It wouldn't hurt to have a few more on hand in case of . . . ah, emergencies."

"Dinner will be ready soon, so don't be too long, dear," Madre said, taking charge. "Before you leave, we'll need to bring the food in from the car."

The family members scattered to do her bidding. Soon everyone, except Dev and Kristi, was reassembled in the shaded courtyard, holding glasses of iced tea and munching on homemade nachos and salsa, while Duke taught his son the fine art of barbecuing ribs.

The Baron stood up and limped over to stare down at Dare, his face stern. "I warned you that you'd break your neck if you kept pulling those fool stunts."

Casey gasped at the Baron's cruel words and shot to her feet ready to do battle. Madre placed a restraining hand on her arm and gave a warning shake of her head.

Dare leaned back in the wheelchair and folded his arms across his chest. "Does my being in a wheelchair make you happier?"

"I never wanted this." The Baron's lips began to tremble, and he hastily wiped them with a hand that also trembled. "Maybe now you'll stop running around the country and start taking an interest in the business." Abruptly he turned away, standing with his back to his son.

Dare stared at his ramrod-straight back, suddenly realizing how upset the Baron was because of his accident. Dammit, he thought helplessly, he wished he knew what to say to his father to make him feel better.

Duke set the tongs on the barbecue cart and walked over to Dare's chair. "You know I'd welcome your help anytime," Duke said softly so as not to startle the baby. "There's more than enough work to keep us both busy."

"Oh, no, you don't," Madre said, her concerned gaze moving from her husband back to her daredevil son. "As soon as you're ready to settle down, Darrick, I hope you'll take over the ranch. I'm ready to hand over the reins."

Dare smiled at his mother, thinking she was a

marvelous woman. Madre, who had been the daughter of the King's foreman, had taken over managing the ranch when her father had died shortly after her marriage to the Baron. It was thanks to Madre that they still had the ranch, Dare knew, and he only hoped he'd do as good a job when he finally took over—if he took over.

"Well, hang in there for a while longer, Madre. You may get your wish."

"You mean you're planning to give up fighting oil-well fires?" Madre asked hopefully, taking the words out of Casey's mouth.

"We'll see how things work out," Dare told his mother, wishing he could give her a more definite answer.

The Baron swung around and glared at his son again. "You should have taken over from your mother years ago. Instead you had to sink your inheritance from your grandfather into buying his half of the Boone Blowout Control Company."

"Only because you were determined to sell it."

"Well, it was losing money. It had always lost money. The only reason Boone could put food—"

"Dad, that's enough," Dare warned.

"Hmmph. First your mother looked after his family, then you took over."

"Dear, now isn't the time—"

"It's past time that someone told Casey the facts of life."

Casey looked at the two men in dismay, realizing that *she* was the reason for the tension that always flared between them. "I knew we were poor—" Casey began.

"Because in the good times your father never put anything aside for the bad," the Baron interrupted, pointing a stern finger at her.

"Dad, that's enough," Dare said, his voice brooking no argument. "The Boone Blowout Control Company is none of your business, but if you'll push my chair down to the stables, I'll be happy to explain a few things to you."

"What was the Baron talking about?" Casey asked Madre an hour later as she carefully piled whipped cream on Davie's christening cake.

Madre rinsed a tomato under the tap, then held it in her hand as she gazed thoughtfully at Casey. "I'm not sure, Casey. The Baron has always been envious of the close relationship Darrick had with your father. It was mostly the Baron's fault. He kept shoving Darrick away." Madre began chopping the tomato. "And after the one big blowup when Darrick was eighteen—when he bought into your father's company—he has refused to fight with his father. Which has made the Baron even madder. He's always wanted to control his sons, but each in his own way has done his own thing."

"I don't know how you've managed it, Madre," Casey said in admiration. "Kept peace in the family, I mean. They are four very proud, very stubborn men."

"I wouldn't have it any other way." She scraped the tomatoes off the cutting board on top of the greens in the smoked-glass salad bowl. "It's so good to have them all home again—even if it had to be on the Rocking R. Thank you, my dear, for inviting us."

"I'm sorry I couldn't convince Dare to go home. He didn't want you to see him in the wheelchair."

"I know. Do you—" Madre put down the paring knife and pressed her fingers to her trembling lips. "Do you think Darrick will walk again?"

"I . . . yes."

"Casey?"

Casey stepped closer to the woman she'd loved as much as her mother and hugged her. "I hope so," she said, wishing she could say something more reassuring.

"I don't know what he'll do if he can't walk." Madre took a deep breath and managed a smile. "He's so impatient. Has been since the day he was born on an offshore rig because he couldn't wait for me to fly back to hospital."

They laughed softly and hugged each other again before returning to their preparations.

"And he's never stopped running since, except for the year he spent in bed. The year he was nine. The year you were born," Madre continued as she mixed the dressing for the salad. "Thank goodness you came along, honey. I think you were the only reason he didn't go crazy. He would play with you for hours, and if he couldn't sleep, he'd hold you and brush your cheek. The next time I'd go into his room, he'd be sound asleep, and so would you."

So that was why it had felt so familiar when he'd stroked her cheek the night before, Casey thought. That's why she'd felt so safe, so loved.

"What was the matter with him?" she asked, realizing that although she knew Dare had spent a year in bed, she had never been told the reason.

"He broke a couple of vertebra in his back. We were afraid he would never walk again."

"Oh, dear." Casey stared at Madre in dismay. No wonder Dare had been so terrified when he'd regained consciousness.

"I think that's why he was always pulling those daredevil stunts," Madre said softly. "Taking those crazy risks. I kept praying he would stop before it was too late."

"Well, it isn't too late," Casey said, resolutely pushing her own doubts aside. "Dare is going to walk again, if it's the last thing I do."

SEVEN

Dare watched as the Lincoln Continental and Ford pickup truck disappeared into the lane, then smiled at Casey, who was standing beside him under the arched entrance to the courtyard.

"Thanks, princess, for inviting the family over. I enjoyed the day. What with one thing and another, it was the first time the family's been together in years."

"I hope it won't be the last," Casey murmured, thinking how lucky she was to have grown up with the three King brothers. Dev and Duke had their own special women in their lives now, but they still made her feel as if she were part of the family. Thankfully, neither Kristi nor Marnie was jealous of her relationship with their husbands, and if things were different between Dare and herself, she could see them all becoming one happy family.

But she and Dare did not have a future together, Casey reminded herself even as she cast a longing glance at his lap. With a sigh, she raked her hair up over her ear and held it there, lost in thought.

Dare gazed at her, aching to reach out and pull her down on his knee, where she belonged. All she had to do was tilt her head and smile at him, or brush her hair up like that, or moisten her red lips, and he wanted to put his ring on her finger. There was no damn way he could attend a family gathering if Casey was there with Morton.

"Is it true, Dare?" Casey asked. "Are you planning to take over the ranch?"

Dare hesitated a moment before replying. "I had always thought that one day I'd wind up running the Regent. I sure can't see myself cooped up in an office."

"Then why, in heaven's name, did you buy into Dad's company?"

"It was just a fluke. Cas was servicing one of King Oil's drilling rigs, and I went along for the ride, then hung around while he went into town for some parts. When the well blew, I had this crazy urge to find out why, so I walked up to it. I spotted the trouble pretty quick and decided to fix it before it caught on fire."

"Which you did, while everyone else was heading for cover," Casey added with a shiver, having heard part of the story before.

"Yeah, I was too dumb to realize the danger. When your dad came back he would have whomped me if he'd been big enough. Instead he asked if I wanted a job for the rest of the summer. By the next day, I was hooked. It's dirty, back-breaking work, but there's something about pitting yourself against the destructive forces of nature that grabs a man—or at least grabs me. Nothing gives me a greater high than taming a wild well before it kills someone. Because that's the bottom line, Casey. That's what keeps me going from one job to the next. No well is worth a man's life."

Hearing the pain in his voice, she quickly stepped behind the wheelchair and gave him a hug. He caught her hands and held them in silence.

"But feeling that way, you'd quit?" she asked, still having difficulty believing he would. Her father hadn't, even though she'd begged him to countless times. And she'd begged Dare to quit too. On their wedding day. Surely if he were serious about quitting, he would have done so then. No. Dare was a *daredevil.* He loved flirting with danger. He would never be content with safe and secure.

"When the time's right," he said quietly. "When I'm ready and on my terms." Releasing her hands, Dare gripped the tires of the wheelchair. "If I'm not trapped in this blasted chair for the rest of my life," he muttered before he could stop himself.

"You'll walk again, Dare. You'll be back fighting fires before you know it." She gave him another hug, then walked into the courtyard. He didn't follow, and she turned to find him still in the archway, looking at the stables.

"What did you say to your father?" she asked thoughtfully. "When you came back from the stables, he was happier than I've seen him in ages."

"I told him that I loved him," he said softly.

"Oh, Dare."

He wheeled the chair around and looked at her, a rueful smile on his lips. "It was long overdue. I have this bad tendency to take it for granted that the people I love know I love them. I guess it doesn't hurt to tell them."

Casey stared at Dare, her lips parted, wondering if, after all these years, he was going to tell her that he loved her. Please don't, she begged silently, because she didn't know what she would say if he did.

He opened his mouth, then clamped it shut and sat, stone-faced, glaring at his clenched hands. Giving a soft sigh, Casey turned away and began plucking the dead roses off a nearby bush. In a week it would be ten years since she'd fallen in love with Dare, Casey remembered. On her sixteenth birthday.

He had taken her to her first dance the night before because Rich had decided she was too tall for him and had weaseled out of their date. Although she'd always been taller than her classmates, her height hadn't normally bothered her; she'd always had to look up at the men she'd admired. This, however, had been different; it was her first real date. Her first homecoming dance. She'd even bought a new dress and high heels for the occasion, and Rich's desertion had hurt.

Dare had found her in her hideaway, had pried the story out of her, then had insisted she go home and get gussied up. The look on his face when he'd picked her up that night made her feel that she was finally a woman.

He danced with her every single dance—to the envy of her girlfriends—flirted with her, and treated her to a hundred of his devastating smiles. But he left her at her door without kissing her.

He returned the next day to lean against the doorjamb, one arm behind his back, his Stetson perched on the back of his head.

"So, princess, you're sweet sixteen today," he said, smiling down at her.

Her head was still in the clouds after spending the night dancing with the most handsome man in the world, and all she could do was stand there and smile at him.

One of his eyebrows shot up. "And never been kissed?"

"Yes," she whispered expectantly.

Slowly he bent his head and kissed her. The moment his lips touched hers, Casey knew things would never be the same between them. No longer could she think of Dare as an older brother, not when his lips felt so right against hers. Not when her heart was so full of joyous wonder, she was afraid it would burst. Not when she loved Dare as a woman loved a man.

He raised his head and stared down at her, his eyes heavy-lidded, a stunned expression on his face. He half bent his head, then raised it.

"Ah . . . ah. Here." He shoved a beautifully wrapped box into her hands, then shoved his own hands into the back pockets of his jeans.

Quickly she tore the paper off the box, and found another doll.

"Don't . . . don't you think I'm too old for dolls?" she asked, trying to keep the disappointment from showing in her face.

"No, princess," he said huskily. "You'll never be too old for dolls."

He had continued to give her a doll for her birthdays—even after she'd left him standing at the altar—but he had never given her his love. Which, Casey told herself firmly, was just as well, because now she understood fully what the cost of loving Dare—of having his babies—might be.

No, Dare, she thought, blinking her lashes furiously as she plucked a rose bud from the bush. Don't tell me you love me. Not now.

Dare watched her massacring the rosebush, his teeth clenched tightly to keep back the words he longed to say. Casey, after all, had told him frequently and in many different ways that she loved him.

He remembered the first time she'd told him. On Valentine's Day when she was five. She'd crawled up on his knee and given him a heart she'd cut out of red construction paper. It had been more of a circle than a heart, but she'd trimmed it in lace and had painstakingly copied a verse on the inside.

He'd hugged her, too tongue-tied to say anything, even when she reached up to kiss him and whispered, "I love you. Will you marry me?"

He'd spent the next ten minutes trying to explain why they couldn't get married, but he hadn't told her that he loved her. Nor had he told her on the many other occasions she'd given him "her heart" and her love. He hadn't even told her that afternoon, by the springs, when they'd made love . . . when he'd finally asked her to marry him.

Nor could he tell Casey he loved her now. Not when there was a good chance there was another man in her life. Not when he didn't know whether he could walk again. Not if he was going to be a burden on her. Somehow he had to keep Casey from guessing how he really felt about her!

Dare cleared his throat, conscious that minutes had passed while he and Casey had been lost in their own thoughts. "Anyway, I also told the Baron that he'd better get off his duff and do something for someone," he said, his voice still hoarse.

She turned and looked at him. "What do you mean by that?"

"It was something Madre told me the year I was lying in bed, feeling sorry for myself." He gave

Casey a lopsided smile. "Actually, I didn't have any choice. She put you in my arms and told me to look after you."

"And you've been looking after me ever since," Casey said softly. Crossing the courtyard, she gave him another hug, then rested her cheek against the top of his head.

"I would have gone crazy if it hadn't been for you," Dare said after a moment. "That's what I meant the other night when I told you that you'd wiped out all your debts the day you were born."

Casey's eyes filled with sudden tears, and she closed her lids tightly, trying to keep them at bay.

For the first time in her life she was thankful she'd been born!

The feeling was so overwhelming, she didn't know what to do—except hug the man responsible. Once again, she hugged Dare. When she was sure her tears were under control, she opened her eyes, raised her head, and stepped back.

He turned and smiled up at her. "Let's go down to the stables. I want to make sure Rebel has settled in."

Rebel was in the stall nearest the door, and Casey choked back a cry of protest as Dare opened the gate and slowly rolled the chair into the stall. The black Arabian stallion snorted, danced away, and pawed the straw on the floor, looking every inch the renegade no one but Dare had ever ridden.

"Easy, boy, easy," Dare said softly, raising his hand. "Come, see me."

Hesitantly, the quivering horse stepped closer, nuzzled Dare's hand, then stretched his head out to stare into Dare's eyes. "It's okay, boy. This confounded chair isn't going to hurt you," Dare said, and continued to speak quietly in his deep, reassuring voice until Rebel finally lowered his head and nosed the rubber tire. "Good boy."

She needn't have worried, Casey realized as she watched Dare stroke Rebel's proudly arched neck with his big hand. There was a special bond between the man and the horse, forged by mutual trust and need. Dare had explained his need one day when he'd been trying to make excuses for her father. After capping a runaway well, the men were charged up, high on adrenaline. Most of the crew headed for the nearest watering hole or gambling den, but Dare unwound by taking Rebel out for a run.

It was that kind of conduct that had made Dare special in her eyes. He stood head and shoulders above all the men she knew, morally as well as physically.

"Lord, I missed this big guy," Dare said, looking at Casey over his shoulder. "And I want to ride him again. Right now."

"You can't," Casey cried out before she could stop herself.

"I thought *can't* wasn't in our dictionary."

"But, Dare, you're still in a wheelchair." She

clasped her hands together, trying not to wring them. "Wait a bit until your legs are stronger and you're not in so much pain."

"I'll go crazy if I have to spend another hour in this damn chair."

"It's too dangerous!"

"I'm going to ride him, with or without your help," he said with quiet determination. "What will it be?"

"What do you want me to do?" Casey asked, capitulating suddenly, knowing Dare was stubborn enough to try to ride Rebel no matter what.

"You could bring me my bridle, saddle, and a rope for starters. Then we'll sort things out as we go."

"What am I going to tell your mother if you get trampled?" she muttered as she handed Dare the bridle.

Dare laughed as he began pulling it over Rebel's head. "Tell her you didn't have a choice. She'll understand."

Perspiration broke out on Dare's forehead, and seeing it, Casey realized he was hurting again. Badly. She quickly lifted the saddle and started to move past him into the stall, but Dare stopped her.

"You hold Rebel. I'll handle the saddle." He handed her the reins, then swung the saddle onto Rebel's back, his teeth clamped tightly to keep back the curses.

Casey swore for him as he tightened the cinch. He wiped the perspiration out of his eyes, then looped the rope over the rafter and began climbing it, hand over hand. Holding the horse steady, Casey watched in admiration as Dare's powerful deltoids rippled beneath his shirt. Moments later he'd lifted his body high enough into the air that his boots were touching the saddle. He tried to open his legs, then cursed in pain and frustration as his muscles cramped, refusing to respond. Quickly, Casey stepped forward, placed a hand on his thigh, and guided him into the saddle.

He sat slightly slumped but upright, smiling in triumph. Then he looked down at his dangling legs. He grunted as he tried to move them. Without giving him a chance to protest, she leaned over and placed his foot into the stirrup. Tears blurred her vision, and head down, she walked around Rebel to secure Dare's other foot. His hand touched the top of her head, forcing her to look up. Blinking back the tears, she gave him a misty smile.

"Thanks, Casey," he said, his voice husky. "I couldn't have done it without you."

"How . . . how does it feel?"

"Fantastic."

The smile he gave her echoed his words, and she drew in a ragged breath, trying to keep her emotions under control. Dare would kill her if she burst into tears. "T-terrific. I'll open the gate and you can ride around the exercise ring."

"Don't bother. I'm going to ride the range."

"Dare—"

"Casey."

"Would you at least wait until I saddle Sundancer," she said over her shoulder as she strode toward the back of the stable. "It will be like old times, riding the range with you."

Dare walked Rebel out of the door and waited in the late-afternoon sunshine, his head thrown back, enjoying the warmth on his face. He breathed deeply, the smells of horseflesh, sun-soaked earth, and cured hay making him feel as if he were alive again. Contentment, pure and simple and almost complete, seeped into him as he looked across the white-fenced paddocks at the rangeland beyond. It stretched to the horizon, where it merged into the Regent Ranch. Lord, how he loved this land.

But not as much as he loved Casey, he thought, smiling at her as she joined him. She looked completely at home in the saddle, her slim body curved gracefully over Sundancer's proudly arched neck.

"I'll race you to the springs," he said, "and if I win, I'll know you're holding back. You and Sundancer have always beaten us."

"We'll *walk* to the springs," she said, and reached out to take his hand.

His smile widened at her sneakiness, but he held on to her hand, enjoying the way it felt in his —so strong, but soft. As the horses pranced along he continued to smile at her, loving the way the sunlight caught in her glorious hair. Loving the rich, brilliant green of her eyes. Loving her.

Casey gazed at the man beside her, totally unwilling and unable to take her eyes off him. He sat tall in the saddle, held there by sheer willpower, she suspected. But oh, he looked so good up there. Where he belonged. On the horse he loved, riding across the land he loved.

With the woman he loved?

Three years earlier she had allowed herself to believe Dare loved her—for a brief few weeks—because even though he hadn't said the words, he had made love to her.

At the springs.

They reached the stand of trees that sheltered her hideaway. Releasing his hand, she led the way through them to the small patch of clover surrounding the springs. He joined her in the clearing, and together they looked down at the water, which bubbled up then gurgled back into the earth.

Their gazes locked for long moments as the memories returned.

Overhead a mockingbird sang a happy song. Casey gave a soft little laugh, and suddenly they were both thinking of the next-to-last time they'd been there. . . .

"What are you doing here?" Casey whispered in delight as she looked up from her notes and saw Dare towering over her library cubicle. He was smiling that special smile, and his warm gingerbread eyes looked good enough to eat. His beat-up, old Stetson was perched on the back of his too long, but nicely mussed hair. A tan cowboy shirt clung damply to his wide chest, and the soft denim of his tan jeans was well worn in . . . interesting places, Casey noted as he stepped around the side of the cubicle. All in all, Dare was the most gorgeous man in the world and a welcome sight for her study-sore eyes.

"You were in Oklahoma when we spoke on the phone last night," she added softly as he stood there and smiled at her.

Man, his princess was pretty, Dare thought, his gaze sweeping slowly over her. But he'd been right the night before in thinking that Casey needed him. Her eyes were too bright. Her shoulders too tense, and her hair was more tumbled than normal, as if she'd been running her hands through it.

"You sounded uptight," he told her in answer to her question. "So I thought I'd come and take you away from all of this." He waved at the stack of books on the desk.

"But I have a final tomorrow."

"Which you'll pass with flying colors if you don't drop dead from exhaustion. Come on." Reaching out, he captured her hand and gave it a tug. "Or I'll pack you out of here over my shoulder."

"You wouldn't da—oh, yes you would."

Laughing, she stood up and clutched her notes to her breast with her free hand.

Dare took one look at her sea-green sundress,

with its wraparound bodice and thigh-hugging miniskirt, and whistled softly. "Wise choice, princess. That dress is barely decent."

"But it's cool," she said, still laughing as Dare hauled her out of the library. It was so good to see him, to be with him again.

He hustled her into his Ford truck. She sat sideways, one knee crooked under her, her sandals dangling from her bare toes, and gazed at him with sparkling eyes while she laughed and talked non-stop all the way to the Regent Ranch.

She was still talking while he saddled and mounted Sundancer, then lifted Casey up in front of him. Still laughing when he set her on her feet next to the springs. Charged up with tension, she danced through the clover, barefoot, her head tilted sideways, her arms outstretched, the sunlight and shadows flashing on her long, golden legs.

Dare remained in the saddle—too aroused from the sweet torture of having Casey sit on his lap to move—and watched her dance, wanting to dance with her but afraid even to touch her for fear he wouldn't stop. Never had he ached to make love with a woman as much as he ached to make love with Casey.

When he'd finally recovered some semblance of control, he dismounted. Wiping his damp hands on the sides of his jeans, he ground-hitched Sundancer, then loosened the cinch. He groaned softly, wishing he could loosen the clothes that were cinching him too tightly.

Casey stopped dancing and looked at him. "Are you okay?"

"Yeah, I'm fine," he said as he spread a blanket on the ground.

Casey sat down, drew up her knees, and tried to cover her legs with her skirt. Giving it up as a lost cause, she stretched out her legs and, pretending it was a pair of shorts, tucked the skirt around them. "Oh, how I wished Dad still owned the ranch. Do you think the owner will mind us trespassing?"

"The old coot's probably off somewhere on a deserted island, cavorting with a beautiful woman. He won't even know we're here," Dare reassured her as he stretched out beside her. He propped his head on his hand and studied her with loving eyes. She was wound up so tight, he was afraid she'd fly apart. Somehow he had to find a way to help her unwind.

"I can't imagine anyone buying a ranch and not living on it," Casey mused, absently twirling a strand of hair around her finger.

"Well, he's letting Madre lease the land, and she's keeping the house aired out, so maybe he'll show up one day. Meanwhile this place is ours."

"It will always be our special place no matter who owns it." She frowned as a huge yawn split his face. "I'm glad you brought me here, but you should be in bed. When was the last time you had any sleep?"

Lifting his hand, Dare covered his second yawn. "Can't remember."

"Well, you should at least take a nap."

"I don't want to miss a moment of your company." He patted the blanket, smiling at her guilelessly, hoping she wouldn't catch on to what he was doing. "But I'll take one if you'll lie down here beside me."

"That's out-and-out bribery."

"Yeah, and I ain't apologizin', princess. Come here."

Laughing, she scooted over and snuggled up against his broad chest, her arm and leg draped over his side, her head on his shoulder. "Is this close enough?"

He shifted his hips and wrapped his arm around her, pulling her even closer until her breasts were flattened against his chest, her pelvis brought smack up against his.

"Now that's more like it."

For an instant she stiffened, then relaxed. This is my buddy, she thought as she breathed in the familiar scent of sandalwood, heard the reassuring beat of his heart. Besides, she loved him. Loved him. Loved him. Loved him.

The words echoed the rhythm of his heartbeat. Gradually his breathing slowed, grew more steady, his arms relaxed slightly, and she knew he slept. Gradually the tension inside her also eased, her mind stopped whirling, and she drifted off to sleep, still thinking, *I love you.*

"I love you." The whispered words woke Dare, and he opened his eyes to find Casey lying on top of him—thigh to thigh, belly to belly, chest to chest. Her elbows were planted on either side of his neck, her chin was propped on her folded hands and she was gazing at him, her green eyes dazzling with gold.

She bent her head and whispered against his lips, "I love you." Then raised her head again.

Suddenly there was no air left in his lungs. He drew in a shallow breath, afraid to breathe, but desperately needing air. His heart began tapping like a runaway pump and something began singing in his ears. A mockingbird, he realized, singing a love song to its mate.

Bewitchingly she smiled at him and repeated again, "I love you."

He stared at her, trying to stay calm, trying to stay rational. Trying not to take what she was offering and run with it to the heavens. "Casey!" he whispered, his voice deep and gravelly. "You haven't told me that since you were sixteen."

"I know . . . because that's when I realized I loved you the way a woman loves a man . . . and I was afraid you would keep thinking I was a child if I kept telling you I loved you every time you came around." Framing his lean jaws with her hands, she smiled down into his eyes. "But it's time—way past time—to tell you again that I love you."

Lowering her head, she kissed him . . . and

once more she was overwhelmed by how right it was to be kissing Dare. His lips felt so right—so warm, and firm, and masculine as they responded to hers . . . then softly, subtly demanded more. His body felt so right—so hard, so solid, and just the right height. Her body fit his in all the right places. Would it fit in all the right places if they made love?

The thought stayed with her . . . tantalizing her, tempting her . . . while his lips made her heart thrum, made her blood hum. While his body made hers ache with need.

Raising her head, she whispered, "Please, Dare, make love to me."

He gazed up at her, his eyes velvet brown with desire, his lips moist with her kisses. "I shouldn't, Casey. Not yet," he said huskily, his words barely audible over the mockingbird's song. How could he keep his wits about him when they were reeling from her kisses? How could he resist her when her body was so tempting? How could he not make love to Casey when he'd been wanting to make love with her for such a long time?

"Why not?" she asked, feeling brazen but not the least bit ashamed. "I'm twenty-two years old. A woman now."

"Oh, Casey, Casey," he said, shaking his head.

The aching tension inside her became almost unbearable, and she moved against him, wishing she were a cat so she could curl around Dare again and again until she was purring with satisfaction.

A second later she was lying on her back, her pelvis cushioning the solid, seducing weight of his. Her insides began to quiver as she felt the heaviness of his arousal, its pulsing heat, which burned through their clothing and into her body. Suddenly she realized her skirt was rooked up so high it barely covered her, and his jean-clad legs felt exciting against her bare thighs.

He raised his pelvis slightly, brushed it against hers, then grinned a naughty, knowing grin that thrilled her to the toes.

"So, you're all grown up? Let me see," he teased as he began loosening the tie that held her top closed. He slipped one long, broad forefinger under each side of the bodice and slowly peeled it back, then gazed down at her full breasts, still covered by an apricot satin-and-lace bra. With one finger, he traced the heart shape created by the lace.

The look in his eyes—the smoldering hunger, tempered with the I'm-not-so-sure-I-should-be-doing-this concern—made her heart skip a beat. Even the touch of his finger made her gasp, made her squirm, made her want more.

Reaching under her back, she unhooked her bra, then gave him a wide, inviting smile. Ignoring the invitation, he slowly slid the straps of her sundress down, his fingers whisper soft as they caressed the sensitive skin along the insides of her arms. Then just as slowly he slipped the straps of her bra down too.

She caught her breath, waiting impatiently for the moment when he would look at her breasts. Would he like what he saw?

His lips quirked in a lazy smile as his thumbs found her nipples, flicking them gently, stroking them through the thin layers of nylon until they were hard and throbbing . . . and so sensitive, she couldn't stand it any longer. Her hands reached for his, but he caught them, holding them as he bent his head and captured a nipple with his lips. He kissed it, nipped it with his teeth, then pressed his mouth down around it into the softness of her breast.

She gasped and moaned, and when the tugging motions of his mouth created a powerful pulsing in her womb, she tried to wiggle away. He trapped her with his strong legs, anchored her with his hard pelvis, and continued to suckle one breast, then the other until her whole body was throbbing.

Finally he raised his head. Releasing one of her hands, he hooked the bra away.

"Casey, princess, you are so . . . so . . ."

Words failed him, but he gazed down at her in adoration, making her feel so very much a woman. Making her want him so very, very much.

Dare shook his head, almost overcome by the sheer beauty of her breasts, their lush curves, the rosy nipples. "Yes, Casey, my little buddy, you have truly grown up," he said huskily. Lowering his head, he kissed her breasts again and again and again. The feel of her soft skin against his lips and the taste of her sweetness in his mouth made his throat ache, made his whole body ache with wanting. Opening the bodice of her sundress wider, he trailed more feverish kisses down her tummy to the top of her panties. His tongue darted under the waistband, making her gasp. Another swipe of his tongue left her shivering . . . and him trembling.

"They have to go," he murmured as he placed another hot, openmouthed kiss into the scrap of satin that covered her.

She caught his hands, begged breathlessly, "No. Please. You're wearing too many clothes."

He lifted his head and looked at her, his eyes smoldering with desire. He blinked, took a deep breath, then raised up higher, bending over so she could reach him. Fervently she ran her fingers across the front of his sweat-dampened shirt, found the buttons and began releasing them, starting from the bottom and working up. Underneath, his skin was warm and moist, roughened by silky hair. Weaving her fingers through the thick, curly hair, she found his hard nipples. She stroked them, then raised her head to plant a kiss, first on one then the other.

A gasp of air whistled through his teeth. "Casey!"

"Yes?" She looked at him demurely from under her thick lashes, her green eyes flashing with mischief.

"That's enough."

"No, it isn't."

"You're right." With a quick shrug, he shed his shirt, then rolled off her to shuck his boots, socks, and jeans. Clad in white briefs, which covered too much of him to suit Casey—but left little to the imagination—he returned to her side. A second later the only thing that shielded her from his ardent eyes was a pair of apricot satin panties.

"You, sweet Casey, have the longest, sexiest legs in Texas! And I'm going to love every inch of them."

He began at her knee, pressing a trail of kisses along the inside of her thigh. By the time he reached her panties, she was panting and squirming, and when he slid his tongue under the lace leg band, she gave a breathy, little cry of need. He continued along the lace, his lips touching the skin beside, his tongue bathing the skin underneath. And with every kiss she crooned and sighed, until her song rivaled the mockingbird's.

When she couldn't stand it any longer, she reached out and lifted his head away. He looked at her, his long, curly lashes lowered, a soft, sexy smile on his lips. "But I'll love it even more when your legs are wrapped around me and I'm buried deep inside you."

"Dare!"

"Do you want that, Casey? Be sure. Because if you don't, now's the time to call a halt."

"I want you, Dare."

"Where do you want me?"

"Inside me. Deep. Deep inside." The words freed her remaining inhibitions, and she caught hold of his briefs and slid them down his hard, muscular thighs. His manhood thrust outward, thick and throbbing.

She gasped, and a flash of hot desire swept through her, leaving her weak, and warm, and wet with wanting.

He groaned and trembled, wanting her so badly, he was afraid he would burst. Just in time he remembered to protect her. Lord, he hoped he was carrying something, Dare thought as he leaned over to pick up his jeans. With fingers that shook slightly he found a foil package in his wallet and slipped on the condom, all the while very aware of her big, green eyes watching him. His fingers still trembled as he removed her panties, and for long moments he just knelt between her legs and gazed at the nest of red curls that covered her sweet secrets.

Then he smiled at her, and told her softly, "Oh, darlin', darlin', I've waited so long for this day." Slowly his fingers parted the curls, found the warm, moist flesh beneath, and began stroking her.

"And I've waited so long too," she whispered, loving the way he had called her darlin' in his deep, sexy voice. Loving, also, what he was doing with his magical fingers. How he caressed her, then filled her, then caressed her again and again until every nerve ending was tight and tingling with pleasure . . . and anticipation. Unable to stand the mounting suspense a second longer, she arched against him. "Please, Dare. Please take me," she begged shamelessly, wanting him wildly, passionately, with every fiber of her being.

And he wanted her, she realized as she saw his nostrils flare, his pupils dilate until his eyes were black. Then she saw no more as his head descended and his lips captured hers.

She only felt . . . the tip of his tongue touching her lips as the tip of his hard shaft touched her softness. His tongue probed her mouth, filling her again and again while his manhood teased her . . . taunted her with persistent probes until everything inside was quivering, pulsing, throbbing with yearning. Giving a needy little moan, she lifted her legs and wrapped them around his waist. With a groan of restraint he thrust slowly, ever so slowly, into her.

Her breath caught in the back of her throat, and he murmured an apology, started to withdraw. Clasping her hands behind his neck, she lifted her pelvis higher against him, wrapped her legs tighter, unwilling to relinquish one inch. He felt so good inside her. Never, even in her most daring dreams, had she imagined it could feel so good. And she only felt this way, she knew, because it was Dare who was loving her.

It felt so good to be inside Casey, Dare thought as he held himself still, waiting for her to accept his presence. So good to be loving her. So good to be finally making her his.

He began to move again, slowly, carefully, treating her as though she were a precious gift he didn't want to break. Gently but thoroughly he explored her, savoring every silken inch of the treasure she was giving so freely.

Raising his head, he gazed down at her as he tenderly made her his . . . watching her green eyes sparkle and shimmer with gold . . . listening to her bluesy voice sing to him again and again . . . waiting until she finally gave herself to him, openly, joyously, completely as a woman gives herself to the man she loves. And then he gave himself to her.

He collapsed against her, breathing heavily, and she wrapped her arms around him, holding him tight. Again and again he kissed her, and tears —were they hers or his?—dampened her cheeks.

He loves me, Casey thought. *Dare loves me.* She held the thought as tightly as she held him.

He loved her, Dare thought. Lord, how he loved her.

Even the mockingbird must know how much he loved her because it was singing a song of love. He sighed, feeling happier than he'd ever felt before because Casey was finally his. It was time to make his life complete.

He raised his head and looked down at her. "We're getting married," he told her softly, then smiled when her green eyes turned to gold again. "As soon as we can find a preacher."

EIGHT

He should have taken Casey straight to the preacher, Dare told himself now as he stared blindly at the bubbling springs. Then none of this would have happened. But Casey had convinced him to wait a month. She had exams to write and she wanted to get married in the family chapel, wearing her grandmother's wedding dress and veil, with all his family and their friends present for the celebration.

He'd waited for years for Casey, he'd told himself. Another month wouldn't matter. His willingness to wait had cost him dearly. He'd lost his best friend, Cas. Worse yet, he'd lost the woman he loved. Casey had a new man in her life. All Dare could ever hope to be was her buddy again.

Suddenly he was unable to hide his yearning. It filled his eyes as he looked at Casey. He cleared his throat and started to speak, then shaking his head, he turned his horse around. With a soft word to Rebel, he rode away from the springs and his memories.

Casey caught him at the edge of the woods and rode beside him, glancing at him in concern. The muscles of his jaw were corded, his shoulders hunched forward, his hands braced against the pommel of the saddle.

For one irrational moment she found herself wishing she'd let Dare take her straight to the altar. Then none of this would have happened. Dare would have quit fighting fires and they would have a baby by now. Only fools dared to dream, she reminded herself sadly.

"Dare, are you all right?" she asked when her concern about him finally overrode her caution about expressing it.

"Yeah." He eased back in the saddle, turned his head, and gave her a tight smile. "Lord, it's good to be in the saddle again, to be able to cover the ground without that damn chair. For the first time since the bomb went off, I feel as if I'm in control. I feel free!" He paused, laughed self-consciously. "Sorry, Casey. I'm not doing a very good job of explaining my feelings. But I sure do thank you for making this possible."

"I didn't do much. It was your bullheaded stubbornness that got you up on Rebel."

Dare urged Rebel closer to Sundancer, then reached out to cover Casey's hand, which was resting on her thigh. "But you were there for me. You made it possible. Thanks."

"I'm glad I could help," she said, wishing she could do more. "That's what buddies are for, aren't they?"

"Do you mean it, Casey?" he asked softly. "Would you be my buddy again?"

"Oh, yes. Yes."

She smiled at him, a wide, bright, flashing smile that made him feel lighthearted for the first time since he'd lost her. "Thank God. I missed you, buddy."

His voice was so deep and full of feeling, it left Casey breathless. "And I missed you," she whispered.

"A dozen times a week I'd find myself dialing your number because I wanted to hear your voice. Once, I even found myself on a plane flying halfway across the world before I realized I was flying home to you." He raised her hand and brushed a kiss against her wrist. "So thank you, princess, for being my buddy again."

Casey gazed at him, speechless. Dare had opened himself up to her as he'd never done before. But it wasn't the vulnerable look in his eyes that stopped the questions tugging at her tongue, she admitted honestly. It was her own vulnerability and lack of courage.

Finally, she managed, "Let's go home, buddy."

"How are you feeling?" Casey asked as she entered the living room later that evening. Dare had been quiet during supper, and she knew he must be suffering from the aftereffects of his ride.

"Full." Dare set the book he'd been holding but not reading on the table and patted his stomach. "I'm going to be fatter than a wallowing hog if you keep feeding me this way."

"Your bag of bones could still stand another twenty pounds."

"Bag of bones?" He placed his hand on his chest. "You wound me."

"Stop fishing, buddy. You know you're the best-looking man this side of the Brazos," she said, realizing how much she'd missed teasing Dare.

He managed to look wounded despite his grin. "Not the other side?"

Laughing, she leaned over and gave his shoulders a hug. "That side too." She straightened, but her gaze lingered on his lap. "Ah, I was wondering if being buddies again means I get to sit on your knee?" Her hands flew to her mouth. "Oh, no. I can't believe I said that. I'm too old to sit on your knee."

"You're never too old, little buddy," he said, reaching up to pull her down on his knee.

With a soft laugh, she turned sideways and curled up, resting against his chest, breathing in the unique aroma she had always associated with Dare, a mixture of sandalwood and spice and honest-to-goodness sweat.

"Are you okay? Am I hurting your legs?"

"A lightweight like you? Hurt me. Hell no." What her firm, round tush was doing elsewhere—now, that was another matter. He shifted slightly, easing the pressure, then placed his big hand on her hip.

Absently, she began playing with the brown, curly hair that poked through the laced front of his shirt. "This is nice. Sitting here on your lap, I mean. It's been such a long time."

"Hmmm," he said, brushing his cheek in her soft, luxurious hair. "I've missed this too." His free hand began gently stroking her hair. After a few minutes of pure contentment, he continued, "Casey, I've been sitting here wondering if some of the kids at the hospital might enjoy riding a horse."

Her head flew up and she gazed at him, wide-eyed. "Dare! What a marvelous idea! I can think of a dozen children who would benefit from riding. I wonder if Dr. Bell would go along with it." She squirmed on Dare's lap, barely able to contain her excitement as more ideas hit her. "They could come out for the day with their parents or volunteers, if necessary. They could ride the horses, swim in the pool. Even do exercises. It would be like a camp, and the kids could come and go as often as they wanted."

He gazed into her green eyes, loving the way they sparkled with gold when she became excited.

"Hold your horses, now. That sounds like a full-fledged program."

"It will be. It's what I've been looking for. That something extra I can give to the children. And just think, I could work with the kids and stay right here on the ranch."

He chuckled. "Almost as good as having your cake and eating it too, hmmm?"

"Even better. And you know how much I like cake." A frown creased her forehead as she thought about all the obstacles in the way. "Maybe it's too much to hope for."

"Knowing you, it isn't. Go for it, Casey. You can do it." He gave her an encouraging hug. "I'll help you all I can."

Looping her arms around his neck, she gazed into his eyes. "I know you will, buddy. You always have." She slanted her head and pressed her lips against his, meaning only to give him a brief kiss of thanks. The moment her lips touched his, she forgot all about being brief. Settling instead for slow and sensuous . . . because that was how she felt when she kissed Dare—so sexy, so sensuous, it was a wonder she didn't dissolve into a simmering pool of desire right there in his arms.

If she kissed him a second longer, he was going to explode, Dare thought, but he kept right on kissing her, because calling a stop would be unthinkable. Having Casey in his arms again was heaven. Kissing her again was heaven. And if heaven also contained the unholy pain of wanting her—and not taking her—then so be it. He'd been wanting her all day. Aching with wanting her. A few more minutes wouldn't matter.

He was wrong, he realized as Casey poked her tongue into his mouth and deepened the kiss. An oil well full of wanting erupted through his body, leaving him trembling. Leaving him so hot and hard, he moaned.

"Casey." His hands, which had been holding her to him, began pushing her away.

Reluctant to go, she clung to his lips. "Hmmm?"

"Dammit, Casey. That's enough."

Raising her head, she looked at him, her eyes confused and vulnerable. The look almost destroyed the last of his self-control. But he might hurt her a hell of a lot more, Dare reminded himself, if he crossed the line from being buddy to lover again—then couldn't marry her. Besides, she had Morton, waiting in the wings.

"Look, Casey. I promised the Third only yesterday that I'd keep my hands off you." He stabbed his fingers through his hair. "How the hell can I do that if you keep kissing me?"

Hurt and trying not to show it, she quickly slid off his knee. Feeling like a heel, he let her go. He stuck his hands under his folded arms.

"I'm sorry, Dare," she said, refusing to look at him as she tucked in her shirttail. "I got carried away."

"You can say that again."

Taking a deep breath, she tilted her head, pushed her hair up over her ear, and held it there. "I still want to thank you for giving me such a terrific idea."

He gazed at her, wondering how he could keep her at arm's length when all he wanted to do was pull her into his arms and make her his. "And I still want to help you."

"I'll phone Dr. Bell first thing in the morning. If he likes the idea, we'll start working with the horses."

"I thought you were going back to the hospital tomorrow."

She let her hair fall, shook it into place. "That was before you pointed me in the direction of my dream. We have a lot of work to do before the horses will be tame enough for the kids." Thank goodness it gave her a legitimate excuse to stay home with Dare, she thought as she picked up a magazine and put it in the rack. She didn't want to leave him alone just yet. After all, he'd only been out of the hospital two days. Two days! It seemed like a lifetime! No wonder he was still having a lot of pain. "Can I do anything else for you tonight? A back rub? Shoulder massage?" she offered, trying to sound casual.

"Nope. I'm fine." Even the thought of Casey bending over him while he was lying in bed was more than he could stand. "And, Casey." He paused, waiting until she was looking at him again, then gave her a slow, sizzling smile. "If you still want to remain my buddy, don't come running in to see me tonight wearing one of those sexy teddies. No matter if I holler down the house."

The memory of Casey in her teddy lingered with him for the rest of the night, adding a sweet agony to the pain he was suffering. It didn't help matters, either, when he pulled open the drawer of the bedside stand and discovered what Dev had bought for him to read.

The presence of that "reading material" plagued him for the rest of the week. It made the sight of Casey, dressed in her bathing suit as she worked with him in the pool, all the more tempting. It made the evenings, with her sitting on his knee telling him stories in her sultry, crushed-velvet voice, all the more delightful. And it made the bedtime back rub, which she insisted on giving him, pure torture—despite the fact that she was fully clothed.

Never had he been so aware of a woman, how she felt when she brushed up against him, so soft and huggable, how she smelled—a mixture of wildflowers and whatever cake she was baking, how she looked—so sexy, so sassy, so adorable as she laughed and teased him while they worked, as she coaxed him into doing exercises or just sat and gazed at him during meals.

She had him so totally befuddled, he'd be running six ways to Sunday if he could run.

Instead, he saddled Rebel and let him do the running, thankful he could at least haul himself into the saddle and stay there while the horse moved smoothly under him.

Dare never ceased to amaze her, Casey thought late Saturday afternoon as she paused from brushing Sunset to watch Dare slide off Sunshine. Anyone else in his condition would still be sitting in a wheelchair. Dare, however, was hauling himself in and out of the saddle more times daily than most cowboys did in a month. Thanks to Dare, the intelligent, but temperamental Arabians had learned to accept the presence of a wheelchair, and had learned to stand patiently while he levered his body into the saddle. Thanks to Dare, they soon would be safe for the children to ride.

Not once had Dare faltered in his efforts. Not once had he indicated, by word or expression, how much pain he was suffering. The brass bedstead above his head told her the real story. Every time she saw how much more it was bent, she felt sick inside.

Knowing it would be disastrous even to mention Dare's pain, she had, nevertheless, insisted on giving him a nightly back rub, steeling herself against the havoc it created in her nervous system. The sight of his beautiful, muscular back was enough to make her insides turn to warm honey, and when she touched him, she felt her body temperature rise to the flash point. By the time she finished, she was almost reduced to molten lava from wanting him.

But wanting him was too dangerous, Casey warned herself now as she'd warned herself every night this past week. She wasn't prepared to face the danger of letting Dare back into her life—nor to pay the price. No, she would play it safe. Still . . .

Lost in thought, she continued to brush Sunset as she watched Dare, now in his wheelchair, pull the saddle off Sunshine's back and balance it on his knee. He glanced at his watch, then up at her.

"It's five o'clock."

"Hmmm."

"Don't you think you should get ready for your big date?"

"Date?"

"Yeah." He cocked his head and gave her a funny look as she ambled over to stand beside him, Sunset following behind. "The Third is taking you out tonight, remember?"

"Oh, my gosh!" She threw up her hand, startling Sunset, and quickly turned to quiet the horse. "I'd forgotten all about it." Giving Sunset's neck a final pat, she stepped back to face Dare. "I wish . . ."

"What?"

"That I didn't have to go. It's my—"

"What?" he prompted, smiling expectantly.

"Nothing. I . . . ah . . . I'd rather spend a quiet evening with you. I've run out of steam."

"I never thought I'd hear you admit such a thing," Dare said, reaching out to take the brush she'd been using on Sunset. "Which means you need a rest. From me. So, go." He waved the brush, banishing her. "Get ready. I'll finish up here."

He took his time and had just finished washing up at the kitchen sink when Casey entered the room. He glanced at her over his shoulder, then wheeled the chair around for a good long look. "Princess, you take a man's breath away!"

"You like this?"

She pirouetted slowly on the toes of her white, deerskin boots, showing off her slim-fitting, boot-length, turquoise skirt, with the fringe-lined slit in the side. A belt of silver conchos cinched the matching top to her incredibly tiny waist. The top bloused over the skirt, had fringes for sleeves and a sweetheart neckline that was cut much too low to suit Dare. Especially when she wasn't wearing it for him.

"The outfit is great, darlin', but you're gorgeous." Gorgeous didn't even begin to describe her beauty, Dare thought. The outfit made her eyes greener. Her Arabian red hair fell to her shoulders, looking tumbled enough to tempt a man's fingers. And her moist, red lips begged to be kissed. Instead he took a deep breath and managed a smile.

The slow, sexy smile he gave Casey almost melted her bones, and the way he said "darlin'" was enough to make her go up in smoke. With a hand that trembled, she held out a necklace of turquoise and silver. "I can't seem to fasten the clasp. Would you mind?"

He took it from her, and she bent over him, lifting her hair off her neck. Her skin felt soft and warm against his fingers, and she smelled so fresh and pretty, like a field of wildflowers rippling in the soft west wind. He noticed the little mole on the side of her neck, and suddenly remembered discovering the other one—on the inner side of her thigh. No one, he suspected, had ever seen that secret beauty mark—except him. The thought set his fingers to trembling, making him fumble the simple task she'd asked him to do.

"Dare? What's taking you so long?" she asked.

"I'm all thumbs," he muttered, trying to concentrate on getting the hook through the safety clasp. Thank God he wasn't expected to cap a wild well right now, he thought as he finally hit the hole. Gently he touched her hair, freeing a strand that had tangled in the chain. She tilted her head, smiled at him.

"Do you recognize it?" she asked.

"What?" he murmured, so bemused by Casey, he could barely think of anything else.

"The necklace? You gave it to me for Christmas one year."

He shook his head to clear it. "Yeah, I remember now. I bought it on a stopover in Istanbul."

She glanced at his knee, thought better of it,

and settled for a chair. Pulling it out from the table, she sat down and gazed at Dare, taking in his sweat-dampened denim shirt, his windblown hair, the deep tan that never faded. He was so handsome, she thought, and drew in a deep breath, trying to stem the feeling of longing that was threatening to swamp her.

"You've sent me a gift from almost every country in the world. Not only me. You've sent gifts to all of your family, each one specially chosen. It didn't have to be Christmas or our birthdays or any other special day; the gifts would just arrive out of the blue. Why, Dare?"

"I missed y'all," he said simply, then knuckled his chin. "And I thought about you a lot. Then I'd see something that would seem to say, 'This is meant for Casey . . . or Madre.' It was a way to bring you closer."

"You were lonely, weren't you? I never realized it before."

Casey was getting too damn astute for comfort, Dare thought in dismay. At this rate he'd never keep his feelings hidden from her. Wheeling the chair over to the fridge, he opened the door and poured himself a glass of iced tea. When Casey refused his silent offer, he replaced the pitcher, lifted his glass, and drank.

Casey watched, mesmerized by the sight of his strong throat muscles working, his Adam's apple moving. Why, in heaven's name, did she find it such a sexy sight? she wondered, then forced her mind back to her recent revelation.

"When I was young I thought you and Dad were so lucky. You traveled all over the world, did exciting things, were on a first-name basis with presidents, and sheikhs, and other rich, powerful people. But the summer when I was eighteen—the summer Mama died—and you took me with you, I realized it wasn't glamorous at all. It was dirty, and dangerous, and just plain hard work."

"I should have been shot for hauling you around the oil patch," Dare said softly, "but your dad needed you."

"I know. He was so lost. Right after Mama's funeral, when you had to return to that well in Indonesia, he was in a real bad way. He'd walk around the condo crying because he should have bought it sooner, then he'd disappear for days. When he came back, he would cry some more. I was frantic. I didn't know how to help him. So I sent an SOS, and you came home and took us with you."

"I should have taken Cas with me right after the funeral, but he was in no shape to let loose around a fire." Cas shouldn't have been let loose, period, Dare thought, remembering the mess he'd found when he'd arrived home. And it was only the beginning! The mess Cas had gotten into before their wedding had been a hundred times worse.

Hopefully, Casey would never learn what her father had done. Unfortunately, if she married

Morton, she probably would. Lord, he wasn't looking forward to the fireworks if that happened.

"Dare? Is there something wrong?"

He glanced up, saw the concern shining in her dark green eyes, and shook his head. "I was thinking about how I had to keep beating the men off with a club that summer."

She laughed. "You sure were protective, all right."

Protective! In spades! Laramie had finally taken him aside and told him he'd lose his crew if he didn't shape up. So he'd made it very clear to the men that Casey was his—although she'd never known it—and then had chewed nails all summer to keep from making his words a reality.

Placing his glass in the sink, he turned to face Casey. "I wanted you to go to college, not get tied up with some roughneck. I wanted you to have an education, to be independent of the whims of the oil business. I wanted you to have your dream."

"I remember the arguments we had," she said, smiling softly. "I'd always wanted to be a physical therapist so I could help Mama, and her death left me without a goal in life. You convinced me that I should carry on with my dream, that there were many other people who would need my help. And you were right." Rising to her feet, she crossed the floor and gave him a hug. "Thank you."

"Yeah, well, at the time I never thought you would be looking after me." And he never thought he'd be sitting in a damn wheelchair watching Casey go off dancing with another man.

The front doorbell rang and he chomped down hard on his frustration and jealousy as Casey went to the door, then brought Morton back to the kitchen. The doctor looked very dapper in a khaki silk sport coat and matching slacks. He even had a maroon silk handkerchief in his pocket that matched his shirt. Yeah, Dare thought as bile burned the back of his throat, it looked as if the Third was ready for a heavy-duty date.

Dare nodded. "Morton."

"King. You're looking all done in."

Dare glanced down at his sweat-soaked shirt and dusty jeans. "Yeah. Casey rode me hard today and hasn't cooled me down yet."

"Dare!" Casey laughed, flushing pink with embarrassment.

"You wouldn't consider postponing your date, Morton, so Casey could finish—" Dare paused, his eyebrow raised, a half smile on his lips. "No, I guess you wouldn't."

"You got that right, King."

"Well then, you take care of Casey. And drive safely," Dare said, leveling Morton with a you-step-out-of-line-and-you'll-answer-to-me glare.

"Dare!" Casey said again breathlessly, suddenly anxious to get Miles out of the house before one of the men threw a punch.

"Y'all have a nice time now," Dare told them, laying on the drawl.

"Don't wait up for us," Miles muttered as he took Casey by the arm and urged her toward the door.

"We won't be too late," Casey called over her shoulder.

The only thing that gave Dare any pleasure, as he watched the couple leave, was the fact that Casey, in her boots, was a good three inches taller than Morton.

A few minutes later even that pleasure faded when he caught sight of the calendar. Oh, no, it couldn't be, he thought, cursing the pain that had made him lose track of the days. It was Casey's twenty-sixth birthday, and he didn't have a gift for her.

NINE

Five long hours later Casey thankfully let herself into the house and shut the door on Miles's retreating back. She hadn't realized how boring Miles was. All he could talk about was himself, his patients, and his mother. To make matters worse, he'd asked her to marry him, then had proceeded to tell her why he was such a good catch. He was safe; he wasn't going to run off somewhere and get killed. He didn't want children, and he wouldn't make any demands on her—except that she entertain his guests.

And look after him hand and foot, Casey had realized suddenly, almost choking on her well-done steak, ordered by Miles because rare meat was bad for *his* heart.

How could she have been so blind? she'd asked herself, remembering a few occasions when she *had* waited on him hand and foot. She'd done it naturally, without thinking, because she'd always looked after her mother. But a husband should be different. He should occasionally do something for her. Miles, she suspected, would never even think of doing anything for her—unless he would also get something out of it for himself.

Why, after almost two years of dating Miles, had she suddenly realized the truth about him? she wondered now as she entered the living room.

Dare was dozing in his chair, a book on his lap. Stepping out of her boots, she walked silently to his side and stood looking down at his clean-shaven jaw, his freshly washed hair.

Because she had finally allowed herself to compare Miles with Dare, she answered her own question. Dare had been the measuring stick she'd always used when a potential suitor appeared on the scene. When she'd met Miles, however, she'd been too numbed by everything that had happened to haul out the stick. Well, now she had, and Miles didn't come within a million miles of the mark Dare had made in her life.

Reaching out, she touched his still-damp hair, brushing it back from his broad forehead. And because touching his hair wasn't enough, she let her palm rest against his temple for a moment. When the temptation to kiss his warm, full lips became almost overwhelming, she reluctantly raised her hand.

Dare opened his eyes, smiled his slow, sexy smile that made her heart shimmer with happiness.

"Hello, Casey. You're home early," he said, his voice husky with sleep.

She pressed her hand against her racing heart. "It's late enough," she said, her voice just as husky.

He yawned, stretched his arms over his head, his eyes never leaving her face. "Did you have a good time?"

"Passable," she said, lying. She'd spent every minute wishing she were at home with Dare. "You didn't have to wait up."

"Oh, but I did. Come into the kitchen and I'll show you why."

"Kitchen! A man waits up for me and invites me into the kitchen," she said, striving to lighten her mood.

"Come."

Laughing, she followed him. Her laughter died as she spotted the cake sitting on the table. It was covered with burned sugar icing, a red candle in the middle, but it was lying inside a large mixing bowl, broken into a hundred pieces.

"Happy birthday, princess," Dare said, trying to act as if nothing were the matter with the cake.

"Oh, Dare. You remembered!"

"Not until after you left and I looked at the calendar." He gave her a sheepish grin. "And then I realized you weren't going to get a cake this year because the Baron shocked us all and took Madre off to San Francisco for a week's holiday. So I tried my hand at making one. Unfortunately, when I turned it upside down to cool, it fell out of the pan all over the counter."

Laughing softly, Casey leaned over and hugged him. "Oh, I love . . . it. Thanks, Dare."

"You're welcome, princess," Dare said, tickled by her pleasure. "I figured it would be a shame if you didn't get a cake. You're always baking cakes for other people."

Releasing him, she bent over the cake and drew in a deep breath. "Hmm. Rum and spice. My favorite. You made it from scratch. I know you did, because I don't have a mix in the house. How did you get everything out of the cupboard?"

"I managed to stand up for more than two seconds at a time. See." He pushed himself out of the chair, straightened to his full height, and stood, his legs apart, his arms at his sides.

"Oh, Dare!" With a jubilant whoop, she threw her arms around him and kissed him on the lips, fully, sweetly, and would have kept on kissing him except he staggered under her weight. Quickly she steadied him, then drew back and smiled at him. "It's so good to see you on your feet again, buddy. Another reason to celebrate. You get the plates and forks, I'll get the glasses and milk."

By the time Dare got the plates out of the cupboard, he was thankful to sit down again. It was worth it, though, to see the joy on Casey's face—to have her kiss him. Why was she kissing him, he wondered, when she was going to marry Morton?

Ceremoniously he lit the candle, then waited

expectantly while Casey made a wish and blew it out.

"What about that! You'll get your wish."

"I hope," she said, smiling at him, praying it would come true. If only Dare could walk again, she wouldn't wish for another thing.

Dare relit the candle, then gazed at her with a knowing smile on his lips. "Now wish for something for yourself, Casey. Otherwise the first wish won't come true."

She wrinkled her nose at him, then blew at the candle. This time the flame wavered stubbornly before it went out. Probably because she didn't deserve the wish, Casey decided as she cut the cake and spooned the pieces onto the plates. Why should it come true if she didn't have the guts to go after it? Didn't have the courage to wish for it. Didn't, if the truth be told, even know exactly what she wanted.

Pushing the thoughts aside, she took a bite of cake and savored it slowly. "Hmm, good." Her tongue darted out, catching a drip of icing from her bottom lip. "You can bake me a cake anytime. Thanks, Dare."

Dare took a deep breath, ordering his heart to behave and his loins to stay cool—with poor results, because she licked her lips again. "I . . . I'm glad I could do something for you, Casey. You've done so much for me these last few weeks."

And so he had baked her a cake, Casey thought as she took another bite. It didn't matter that big, macho men weren't supposed to bake cakes. It didn't matter that Dare could barely stand. He had baked a cake for her—and had cleaned up the kitchen. She bet that Miles, on the other hand, had never even seen the inside of a kitchen. As for baking her a cake because she didn't have one? Miles would never even think about it, much less stoop to do it.

And that was only *one* of the reasons she would never marry Miles, Casey thought, smiling at Dare.

Returning her smile, Dare reached out and took her hand, then held it as he continued to eat his cake. It was so good to sit and share this time with Casey, he thought. So good to be able to do something for her and have her appreciate his efforts. He was going to hoard this memory so he could cherish it when he could no longer do things for Casey.

Which would *never* come to pass, he decided suddenly. Even if she *did* marry Morton, he would still do things for Casey. Still give her gifts.

He looked down at his now empty plate, then back at Casey. "I wish I had a present for you."

"Oh, but I do have one. It arrived a couple of months ago. I stashed it away in my bedroom." She raised an arched eyebrow. "I wonder what it might be?"

Remembering, he shot her a slightly apprehensive grin. "Who knows? Maybe I'll surprise you this time."

She stood, crooked a beckoning finger. "Come. Let's see."

Dare followed Casey into his bedroom, rolled across the floor to the window seat, and stared down at the assortment of dolls he'd sent her over the years. Some had china heads, others were made of rags. Some were made to be played with, others were beautifully dressed in national costumes. Picking up one of his favorites, a doll he'd found in a little shop in Scotland, he fingered the tartan skirt.

Box in hand, Casey emerged from the closet and sat on the corner of the bed, facing Dare. The tires swished on the hardwood floor as Dare rolled the wheelchair over to the bed. He sat, watching anxiously as she removed the wrapping paper and opened the box.

"Oh, she's absolutely beautiful," Casey said as she lifted out a doll dressed in a Spanish wedding gown with a lace veil covering her red hair.

He breathed a sigh of relief. "I thought so, too, the moment I saw her, but I debated for days before I bought her. I was afraid I might hurt you." He gazed at her earnestly. "And believe me, princess, that wasn't my intention. I just wanted you to have her."

Carefully Casey laid the doll back in the box, then leaned forward to place it on a nearby chair. "But I can't accept her, Dare. She's an antique. She's priceless."

"That's why she should belong to you."

Reaching out, he captured her hand, drew it to his lips, and brushed a kiss across her knuckles.

She caught her breath, then forgot to breathe while he turned over her hand and planted another kiss, openmouthed this time, on the sensitive inside of her wrist. Heat and moisture from his lips flowed through her, turning her warm and moist inside.

She swayed forward. Catching her by the waist, he lifted her onto his lap. She came willingly, snaking both arms around his neck and smiling at him.

And then he kissed her, kissed her the way he'd been longing to do all night, kissed her the way he'd been aching to do all week—hard, hot, demanding. Showing her, with his lips and his tongue, how badly he wanted her.

Casey kissed him back, her lips soft and pliant—but just as hot and demanding as his. She kissed him the way she'd been longing to do since he'd kissed her in the pool, holding nothing back, not even her sighs or her breathless gasps. Because that was the way Dare made her feel when he kissed her, so breathless, so needy . . . her senses so swamped by him that the world could come to an end and she wouldn't even notice.

Abruptly he pulled back his head and gazed at Casey's lips, now swollen by his kisses. "Dammit," he wheezed, barely able to catch his breath. "I shouldn't be kissing you."

"Why not?" she asked in bewilderment, feeling suddenly lost and needy because he was no longer kissing her.

"Because you're going to marry Morton."

"No, I'm not." She straightened slightly and looked into his eyes. "He asked me tonight and I said no."

"No?"

"Unequivocally no."

He tilted his head and smiled. "Then there's no reason I shouldn't kiss you."

"None," she whispered, too needy to remember the other reasons. Leaning forward, she brushed her lips against his.

The gesture, so warm and giving, shattered the last of his self-control. Lifting her as easily as if she were a doll, he placed her on the bed, then followed, pulling his body up to cover hers. Her laugh of delight was smothered as his lips captured hers again. He plunged his tongue into her open mouth, making her gasp, making her moan, making her writhe helplessly under him. He knew he was too heavy for her, that he was squeezing the air from her lungs, but for a moment he could think of nothing except his overpowering need—to lie on top of her, to feel her softness under him, to be buried deep inside her once again.

Casey was totally engulfed by Dare, so achingly aware of his hard, muscular body as it pressed hers deeper into the mattress. His male heat surrounded her, along with the scent of sandalwood, and the combination did heady things to her nerve endings. His tongue probed her mouth again and again, the erotic motion making her breasts swell, her heart pound wildly, her head spin. His manhood throbbed against her soft mound, and she felt an answering throb begin deep inside. Suddenly she knew that she would continue to throb, continue to ache, continue to feel empty until Dare filled her.

Dare shuddered, fought for control. With a groan he tore himself away from her clinging lips and enticing body. He lay on his side, gazing at her, shaking his head in self-reproach. She stared back, wide-eyed, her chest heaving as she drew in a ragged breath, and for a moment he was afraid he'd frightened her by his unbridled need.

Then she smiled and whispered, "Please, Dare, make love to me."

"Oh, Casey, darlin'. I want to make love with you, but I'm not sure if I can," he admitted softly.

Her smile widened as she slid her hand down the front of his jeans and cupped him. His manhood—already full and aching—strained even harder against the fly.

"There's nothing wrong with your equipment, King," she said in her sultry, sexy, bedroom voice. She gave him another bold caress, felt him respond, and suddenly she knew what she wanted to do. She sat up, feeling so wicked and excited, she could barely keep from laughing out loud. "The last time we made love, you undressed me. This time I'm going to undress you."

He started to object, then caught back the words as he saw the look on her face. She was feeling full of herself. Like a frisky colt wanting to test her newfound power. And there was no doubt about it. She had the power to make his blood run hot, to make him tremble the way the ground trembled when a well was about to blow. So, for now, he'd let her have her power . . . and hoped to high heaven he didn't explode.

He lay back on the bed and gave her a slow smile. "I'm ready and willin', darlin'," he said, his voice rumbling in his chest. "And I'm all yours."

His words thrilled her, filling her to the brim with something she didn't dare to name. Because, once again, Dare was giving to her—this time the gift of his body to do with as she pleased. And all she wanted to do was please him.

Slowly, she trailed her hands across his chest, then began unbuttoning his shirt, glancing at him from beneath her lashes, looking so demure, he could barely keep from laughing. Then all thought of laughter fled as she leaned over and teased his nipple with her teeth. His breath caught in his throat, and he held it, not daring to breathe as she toyed with first one nipple and then the other, lapping it with her tongue, rolling it between her teeth before sucking it into her mouth. He arched his chest toward her, at the same time aching to pull away, wondering if he had enough staying power to last until she was done toying with him.

Finally she took pity on him and raised her

head, giving him a lascivious grin as she began tugging his shirt off his arms.

"You're enjoying this, aren't you?" he said with a growl, lifting his upper body to aide her.

"Very, very much," she whispered, her gaze sliding to his straining fly. "But not as much as you."

He laughed huskily, then caught his breath as she undid his belt buckle and released the top button of his jeans.

She moaned. "Oh, Lord, buttons." A flush of warm blood swept through her entire body from her cheeks to her pelvis, then pooled in her womb. She took a deep breath, trying to keep from melting into his arms, trying to stop her fingers from trembling, trying to concentrate on undressing Dare. "Buttons on the fly of a man's jeans have got to be the sexiest thing I've ever seen."

"They turn you on?"

"Yes," she said on a hiss of air. "They make me all hot and bothered."

"I wish I'd known."

She released another button, gasped, then looked up at him. "Dare! You're not wearing shorts!"

"Somehow I didn't think you'd be giving me a back rub tonight."

"You're right. No back rub, but this instead."

Before he could guess her intentions, she leaned over and pressed her lips into the open vee of his jeans. Heat drilled through him, right to his backbone. His pelvis jerked.

"Casey!"

"Uh-uh, this is my show," she warned as he reached out to her. With a muffled oath, he clenched his fists. Giving him a wicked smile, she released another button. She leaned over him again, warmed his hair-roughened skin with her breath, flicked it with her tongue, then kissed it, hotly, wetly.

He grabbed the rungs of the bedstead, knowing that if he didn't, he'd be pulling her head away, wrapping his arms around her, doing anything to stop the sweet torment. And he really didn't want Casey to stop brushing her fingers against him or touching his skin with her lips . . . or touching him.

The feel of her lips against his throbbing shaft, however, was more than he could take. Reaching down, he raised her head and gazed into her eyes. "No, Casey. Please don't. Not this time."

"The next time, then?" she asked, wondering if there would be a next time.

"Yeah," he promised. If he had his way, the "next times" would continue until he was old and gray.

"Then I guess I'll have to be content with kissing your legs," she said, gazing regretfully at his bulging jeans. "Because if I remember correctly, you kissed mine."

Slowly, ever so slowly, she eased his manhood

out of the blue denim. It was so hard, so heavy, so primed with desire that once again she felt her bones melt, her heart expand, her womb fill with need. She shivered, drew in a shaky breath, then with a lingering brush of her fingers returned to the task of removing his jeans.

She glanced up at him, then smiled as she saw that he was hanging on to the bedstead with grim determination. Lowering her gaze, she continued to pay homage to his manhood as she exposed an inch of flesh, then kissed the insides of his thighs—first one then the other. Exposing another inch, she kissed it too. His thighs were rock hard, but they quivered under the touch of her lips. A heady sense of power filled her, and along with it an aching need to give this big, beautiful man as much pleasure as he had suffered pain.

Sweet heaven, what torment, Dare thought, gripping the bedstead more tightly than he'd ever held it before. Would this agony ever end? How long did he have to lie helpless, at the mercy of the woman he loved?

Thankfully, by the time she reached his knees, she did show mercy and quickly pulled his jeans down to the tops of his boots. She tugged his boots off, shucked his jeans, then turned to look at him once again. Her lips parted and she licked them.

"You, Darrick King, are definitely a sexy, sexy . . . sexy man," she said, her voice becoming smokier with each word. Reluctantly, she raised her eyes above his waist. He was smiling at her, his hand outstretched.

"Come."

"Not yet." Tossing her head, she gave him a slow, smoldering smile, then slipped from the bed. "Now you're going to lie back and watch the show."

"Casey!" His laugh was more of a groan as he realized what she planned next. "I don't know how much of a show I can take."

"Well, I know your staying power, big boy, and you'll take as much as I can give you." Turning out the overhead light, she crossed the floor to the window. She stood in the pool of moonlight, her hands pressed against her stomach, trying to quiet the quivering feeling inside. Then, reaching under the hem of her top, she released the button of her skirt and eased it over her hips.

Arm bent under his head, Dare watched as the skirt slid down her incredibly long, incredibly sexy, black, silk-clad legs. Casey was doing a strip for him, he thought, trying to stem the wild elation rising inside him. Once she had braved a lingerie shop to buy clothes to please him. Now she was stripping to please him. Someday soon, the Lord willing, he was going to claim this wonderful woman for his wife. But not until he could move his legs. Not until he could give her everything she was giving him.

Stepping out of the skirt, she unhooked the silver belt and trailed it through the moonlight to the pool of green at her feet. The necklace then followed the same silvery path. Slowly, sensuously, she began easing her blouse over her head. He waited in breathless anticipation until she stood naked in the moonlight. It spilled over her shoulders to bathe her firm, rounded breasts and kiss the proud peaks.

"Oh, darlin', darlin'," he whispered, then couldn't say anything more because he forgot to breathe.

His gaze lowered, and he sucked in a lungful of air as he realized she was wearing a garter belt and no panties.

"When I got dressed tonight, I was thinking of you," she explained, her voice velvet soft as she released the garter and began sliding the silk stocking down her golden leg.

Her words sent another surge of elation through him. She had dressed for him . . . not Miles. Beneath her beautiful outfit, she'd been wearing the sexiest scrap of lace he'd ever seen . . . for him.

"Next time, darlin', I want to undress you," he said, wishing his hands could follow the moonlight that silvered her breasts and shimmered along her legs. Wishing he could strip back the shadows that hid the secrets at the top of her thighs.

"Perhaps," she said huskily, not sure if she wanted to give up her newly discovered power. It was so thrilling to know she could make Dare want her, to watch the effect she was having on him. He lay in the moonlight, motionless except for his manhood, which was straining erect. He was so bold, so powerful it made her feel warm and receptive inside. Her own actions were also making her feel this way, she knew. Just as she knew that she wasn't being wanton or daring because she was stripping for Dare . . . but loving and giving.

She had so much more to give.

Removing her garter belt, she slowly crossed the room to him and paused at the side of the bed.

He held out his hand. "Lord, but you're beautiful, Casey. I'll never see the moon rise without remembering how you look at this moment, so graceful, so elegant, so very much a woman. And I want you now. I need you now."

"And I need you," she said as she slipped into his arms.

He kissed her lips, her neck, her beautiful breasts, wondering if he could ever get enough of kissing her. His hand caressed her back, her hips, the inside of her thighs, but when his fingers found her warm, damp, intimate folds, he paused.

"Are you protected, darlin'?"

"Nooo," she wailed.

"Dev took care of it for us. Look in the nightstand. You'll find the 'reading material' he drove into town to buy."

She pulled open the drawer and discovered a box. "Condoms." She giggled, half in relief, half in embarrassment. "Let me put it on."

He laughed softly at her daring and nodded, wondering if she would ever stop surprising him.

She opened the foil, took one look, and giggled again. "It's hot pink."

"I'll kill him!"

"No, you won't. You'll thank him for his thoughtfulness. Now lie still."

She touched him, and he shuddered, then held himself very, very still. "Be careful, darlin'. The last time I made love was over three years ago—with you at the springs."

Casey stared at Dare in astonishment. He hadn't been with another woman, she thought in wonder as she began rolling the condom on his throbbing shaft. What a special, special man.

And because he had waited so long, she wanted this time to be special for him. The thought swept away the last of her concerns about whether she could make it good for him. She had the power to pleasure him, to love him . . . to give to him everything he needed, everything he deserved.

Slowly she rose above him, then lowered herself onto him, concentrating on taking him into her body. He felt so hard, so big, so thrilling, she could barely restrain herself from moving over him in feverish delight. When he filled her completely, she looked up at him and smiled.

Dare gazed at her, tight-lipped, afraid to move even one muscle for fear of exploding inside her. She was so velvety soft, so hot, so incredibly sexy . . . and she was Casey, the only woman he had ever wanted, the only woman he had ever loved.

She began moving over him slowly, every cell of her being totally aware of his manhood as it brushed against the sides of her tight tunnel. He throbbed against her softness, making her heart beat wildly, making her realize she was no longer in control.

Once more Dare was giving to her, Casey thought as the bliss built inside her. Giving her a precious gift that only he could give. Suddenly she was so full of his loving that it burst forth in wave after wave, flooding her entire body.

With a cry of wonder, she collapsed against him, and he held her, loving the way her body was contracting around him, loving the way she was coming apart in his arms. Loving the way she was giving herself so unselfishly to him. Then, with a shout of joy, he erupted inside her, giving and giving to her until he had nothing left to give.

Gradually his heartbeat slowed, gradually his breathing returned to normal. Finally he was able to ask, "Are you all right, Casey?"

She nuzzled his sweat-dampened shoulder. "More than all right. I feel stupendous. Oh, Dare, that was so wonderful."

He laughed softly. "Thank you, darlin', for the lovely, lovely gift," he said, feeling as though she had given him the most precious gift in the world.

He stroked her hair gently, then moved his

hand down to brush her silken skin. He could lie there forever if Casey were in his arms.

But only if he could also dance with Casey . . . and that might never happen. He thought about the dances he'd taken her to over the years. The first one—the homecoming dance—when she was sixteen and so shy, she'd spent the whole night with her head on his shoulder, the barn dances and the square dances, where she'd thrown back her head and laughed as he'd swung her off her feet. And the night in Edmonton when they'd slow-danced until he ached from wanting her. He had walked away from her that night, and he'd walk—no wheel—away from her again if he had to. Although he'd stood on his two feet for a few minutes tonight—for Casey—only sheer guts and determination had kept him there. He had a long way to go before he could walk, let alone dance, with his beloved.

Casey lay in Dare's arms, thinking that it had been a very special birthday because Dare had made it so. What he'd done for her tonight topped everything he'd done before. He had given her a very special gift—himself. He had set aside his pride and risked failure, because of her. Had made himself vulnerable, because of her. Had given her complete control over him . . . because he trusted her. Perhaps even loved her? She didn't know. All she knew was that once again, Dare had given her something she'd remember for the rest of her life. And she didn't know what she was going to do with the gift.

"Thank you, Dare, for the doll," she whispered, wanting to thank him for more but afraid of saying too much. "But don't you think I'm getting too old for dolls?"

"No, princess. I'll be giving you dolls when you're celebrating your birthdays from a rocker."

"You said something like that once before," she said, smiling at the memory. "When I was sixteen and thought I was all grown up."

"That was the day I gave you your first kiss." He laughed softly. "Believe me, after that kiss, I *knew* you were all grown up. It shocked the socks off me."

"Then why do you keep giving me dolls?" she asked, wiggling around until she could gaze into his eyes.

"Because I'll never forget your first birthday." With gentle fingers, he brushed a strand of hair off her face. "You'd been invited to another girl's birthday party the day before and had latched onto her doll like a bur. I'd been delegated to bring you home, and when it came time to leave, you gave back the doll without shedding a tear." His thumb touched the corner of her mouth. "It was a bad year in the oil patch, and the ranch wasn't faring much better because of a drought. Your mother was still in the hospital, but Madre made you a pretty dress and gave you a party. You got a few presents, but I remember the look on your face when you didn't receive a doll. It almost broke my heart." He gave her a lopsided grin. "So I rode my horse to town and bought you one exactly like the other girl's."

"With what?" Her eyes grew thoughtful. "You couldn't have had any money either."

He hesitated a moment before admitting, "I traded in my saddle."

"Dare. You did that! For me?"

"Yeah. I figured you were pretty special then. I still do." He gazed at her for long moments, tempted to tell her how much she meant to him. When the temptation grew too strong, he lowered his head and whispered against her lips, "Let me show you, again, how very special you are."

Dare awoke the next morning in a state of pure contentment because he was still holding the woman he loved in his arms. He'd half expected Casey would leave his bed sometime during the night, and had wrapped his arm around her to keep her from moving. Not only had she stayed, he realized, a smile curving his lips, she was pressed against him close enough to be a second skin.

Pressed too closely, Dare discovered a moment later as she wiggled against him. His loins responded instantly. Thank goodness he had no more worries on that score . . . as long as he had a generous woman to love him—as long as he had Casey. No other woman would do.

She woke, moved sleepily against him, then turned toward him. He turned, too, so she wound up lying full length on top of him. She brushed her cheek against his chest, ran her hand down his side —and found his aroused state. Abruptly her head came up and she stared at him, her mouth open. Very carefully, she let him go.

"Mornin', darlin'," he said huskily.

"You're up. I mean awake."

"I'm both."

With a groan of embarrassment, she buried her head against his chest. "You sure are."

Laughing softly, he brushed a hand over her hair. "How are you feeling this fine mornin'?"

She took a deep breath and sighed happily. "Fine."

"But a bit sore, I'd wager." She remained silent, and he continued to stroke her hair. "Don't worry. You won't have to work you wily ways on me this morning. I'll survive."

She raised her head and smiled at him, thinking that he was doing it again—looking after her. "Oh, Dare. I wouldn't mind."

"I know, but believe me, it isn't necessary. In fact, if you're going to get any work out of me today, you're going to have to lay off me, darlin'. I'm too old to be acting like a young buck."

"Old. Hmmph. That will be the day." She dropped a kiss on his lips, untangled her limbs from his, and slipped from the bed. Nonchalantly, as if it were a normal occurrence to stand naked in front of a man, she picked up his shirt and put it on, doing up enough buttons to remain modest.

Leaning on his elbow, Dare admired the way his shirt looked on Casey. It covered her saucy bottom but revealed most of her long, shapely legs, and every time she bent over he could see a lot more of her beautiful breasts than she intended.

"I am nine years older than you, Casey," Dare said gruffly, suddenly aware of the passing of time. Until now he'd been content to wait—until Casey grew up, until she finished college, until he got out from under the staggering debt load he'd been carrying. But dammit all, he didn't want to wait one moment longer. He wanted to marry her immediately and start giving her the babies she wanted—the babies he wanted. Damn these useless legs to hell and back!

"You've always been right for me," she said as she picked up the wedding doll and carried it over to the window seat. She shifted the Jamaican doll to one side and made room for the new doll next to Shy Violet. Walking over to the rocking chair, she gazed down at the Princess, remembering what Dare had told her the night before. Never again would she object when this unselfish man gave her a doll.

"Are you going to let your children play with your dolls?" he asked, picturing their redheaded daughters having a tea party with their dolls.

For a moment Casey allowed herself to dream about a little brown-headed girl, trotting across the floor toward her giant of a father, holding the Princess in her outstretched arms.

Deliberately forcing the dream aside, she leaned over, picked up the Princess, and began fussing with her dress. "I'm not having any children," she said, answering his question.

"What!" He pushed himself into a sitting position and stared at her in shock. "What the devil are you talking about?"

"I'm not going to have children," she repeated, clutching the Princess against her breast, trying to keep the hurt and fear bottled up inside.

"But you've always dreamed of having children. Why did you change your mind?"

"Because I no longer dare to dream. The risk is too great."

"Risk? I don't understand."

She drew in a shaky breath and forced the words past her aching throat. "You know Mama had an aneurysm when I was born. Well, it's hereditary, so there's a . . . chance the same thing might happen to me if I had a child. I . . . decided I couldn't take the risk."

Dare stared at Casey, dumbfounded, trying to make sense of her words. Sure he knew what had happened to her mother; however, he'd never suspected Casey was worried about the same thing happening to her. "But three years ago you were willing to marry me. To have my children."

"Because you railroaded me into a wedding before I had a chance to think."

"I didn't."

"You did. One moment we were making love, and the next you were rushing me to the altar. Thank goodness you're treating me like a woman this time around. Thank goodness you aren't demanding that we get married today."

Which was exactly what he'd be doing, Dare thought ruefully, if he could walk. Hell and damnation!

"And thank goodness," she continued as she wearily pushed her hair off her forehead, "that we didn't get married three years ago. I would never want my children to go through what I did." She drew in another ragged breath. "And my poor mother. When I think about how she must have suffered, how she must have longed for a normal life with her husband . . . I want to cry."

Afraid she might do just that, she turned away and placed the Princess back in the rocker.

Dare gazed at Casey, feeling completely at a loss as to what to say or do to help her. She had always been so courageous. Why was she afraid to take the risk other women in similar circumstances were willing to accept?

Suddenly he realized what this was *really* all about. Suddenly everything he'd ever believed in, everything he'd ever stood for—his whole life—lay in ashes at his feet.

"Casey! Look at me!" he demanded impatiently. Slowly she swung around on her bare heel and stood with her arms folded protectively across her middle, looking so lost and forlorn that he wanted to reach out and comfort her—despite the fact he was hurting so badly that he didn't have one drop of comfort to give. "Did you think, Casey, that I would treat you the way your father treated your mother? Were you afraid that if something happened to you, I would go off and leave you? Is that why you stayed away from me all this time?"

"Yes!" Casey whispered, then repeated louder: "Yes! Yes!"

TEN

Dare passed a trembling hand over his face. "So at least I now know where I stand with you."

No, he didn't, Casey thought sadly, because she wasn't sure how she felt any longer. "When you asked me to marry you, I was so surprised and so happy that I didn't stop to think about what getting married or having children might mean," she said, trying to explain how she'd felt three years earlier. "Then two weeks after Dad's death when I went back to the hospital to finish my practicum, I was assigned to work with a woman who had suffered an aneurysm during childbirth—just like Mama. I kept thinking that it could have been me lying there on the bed." Casey swallowed hard. "Her husband never came to visit, and she didn't get to hold her baby. You see . . . she died."

"Oh, Casey." He held out his arms. "Come here, princess."

She flew across the floor and, with one graceful movement, nestled in his arms. He held her close, brushing his hand over her tumbled hair as he spoke. "I'm so sorry, Casey. I wish I could have been there to help you. To at least talk to you."

"I wish you'd been there too," she whispered against his bare chest. "Maybe I could have kept things in perspective. Maybe I wouldn't have let them build and build in my mind. Maybe I would have been able to conquer my fear. But you weren't there, Dare."

"I wanted to stay with you, princess," Dare said softly. "But I had to kill the well that killed your father, and it took months. By that time . . . when I hadn't heard from you, I figured you'd really meant it when you'd told me that you no longer wanted me in your life."

"And I didn't contact you because I was afraid to let you back in my life. Afraid to take the double risk of marrying you. Losing you to a wild well would have destroyed my soul, but losing you because I was ill . . . would have destroyed my will to live."

"Casey, darlin', if we had gotten married and if, by some horrible turn of fate, you'd suffered a stroke, I would *never* have treated you the way your father treated your mother. The wedding vows say in sickness and in health, and when I make a vow, I keep it."

"Still, I would never want you to go through

what my father did. To spend all those years loving a woman who couldn't love him back."

He should have known how Casey felt, Dare berated himself as he continued to hold Casey. After all, she had every reason to feel as if she had been abandoned by the people she loved. Her mother, through no fault of her own, had abandoned Casey at birth, and so had Cas when it came right down to it. Time and time again Dare had seen her gazing hopefully over his shoulder when he'd come home from a fire, had seen the hope turn to resignation as she realized that Cas hadn't come home with him. Still, it hurt like hell to learn that Casey believed he would also desert her.

"Casey. If you'd told me about your fears, I wouldn't have insisted on having children."

"But I know how much you've always wanted children of your own, Dare, and I would have been totally miserable if I couldn't give them to you. I would have wound up feeling as if I'd failed you . . . failed myself."

He continued to stroke her hair, wishing he could think of something else to say that would convince Casey to take the risk of loving him, of marrying him. Because he would never, ever leave his princess, his buddy, his love. "So where does that leave us?"

"Now that we've made love?" she asked, raising her head to look at him from beneath a curtain of hair.

"It's your call, darlin'."

"Could we . . ." She looked away, then back at him bravely. "Could we be lovers?"

He gave a surprised, pleased little laugh. "Casey!"

"We've been friends and buddies. Now I'd like to be your lover."

"Nothing else?" he pushed, testing.

Sadly she shook her head. "No, Dare."

He hesitated a moment, his gaze lingering on her trembling lips and her bright eyes. "Then I'd be honored to be your lover," he said softly as he lowered his head and kissed her. For now. Until he could walk again . . . and then he'd demand more.

Lovers. Casey slowly savored the word in her mind, thinking of all the ways Dare had made love to her this past week. Turning slightly in the big chair, she looked longingly at her lover, who was lying, boots off, on the couch watching the Cowboys battle the Redskins on *Monday Night Football.* He'd banished her to the chair earlier, telling her sternly that she was a menace whenever she came within two feet of him. And he was right, she thought, a wicked little grin on her lips, but she'd been having so much fun loving Dare.

The brandy-sauce cake she'd served him the night before—on top of her tummy—had been a delicious hit. The night before that, her dance of the seven veils had produced such spectacular results that her body still trembled with the memory of how well he had loved her. Dare was the most caring, considerate lover a woman could ever hope for. And, for now, he was hers—until he was well enough to chase wild wells again.

She shivered, unable to control the feeling of apprehension that clawed at her every time she thought of Dare trying to cap a blowing well—only one spark away from certain death. But as much as she wanted him to be safe, she was still doing her utmost to help him walk again.

He was standing for longer periods, and she was trying to teach him to use crutches. So far, however, he couldn't lift his leg and take a step, couldn't even lift his weight and swing his legs forward. She'd seen the effort he made, seen the frustration on his face, and the pain, and wished she could work magic on his nerves and muscles so they'd heal. But healing took time, and she was desperately afraid Dare wouldn't give himself the time he needed.

A compelling urge to get up and hug Dare swept through Casey, and she squashed it down, knowing where it would lead. Later, she promised herself, after she'd made sure everything was ready for the following day. Thanks to Dare's relentless work—and at what cost to him she could only guess, because never once had he complained—the horses were ready. The kids were coming for the first time. So, unfortunately, was Dr. Bell. With a sigh, she turned her attention again to the checklist.

"I hope tomorrow won't be a disaster," Casey said after she'd checked and rechecked the list. She glanced up and found Dare watching her, with a smile on his face and a look in his eyes that told her he'd been thinking about the previous night and the cake. Of course he'd probably been helped along by the fact that he'd consumed another piece. The empty plate was sitting on his flat stomach, just above his bulging fly. She felt her insides turn to caramel butter and took a deep breath, forcing herself to think about tomorrow.

"You'll do fine," he said, wondering how she could look so innocent, sitting there. Two nights earlier she'd strolled into this very room, wearing an ankle-length cowboy duster—over nothing but a pair of chaps. He forced the memory to the back of his mind, afraid his straining jeans would start popping buttons.

"But Dr. Bell is coming along too," Casey reminded Dare for the tenth time since supper. "I'd hoped we'd have a chance to test out the program before he put in an appearance."

"Well, you can see his side of things. He wants to make sure the kids will be safe."

"I know, but I also get the distinct impression that he doesn't think I can handle the program. That I'm too young to have so much responsibility."

"You've been responsible all your life, and I'll tell him so if you want."

"You'll be there?" She'd fully expected Dare to make himself scarce, knowing how much he detested anyone seeing him in a wheelchair.

"In the background, cheering you on to success," he said as he reached up and put the plate on the end table.

"Oh, Dare, I hope it will be a success." Leaving the chair, she knelt beside the couch, seeking the shelter of his arms. He gave her a reassuring hug then pulled her up to lie on top of him. "I want to work full-time with the children, here on the ranch," she continued after a moment. "It doesn't matter if I don't make much money, I don't need much. The ranch is mine, and the dividends from Dad's share in the company give me a very comfortable living. But I need Bell's official recognition before the Lone Star Hospital will send me their children. If Bell doesn't support the program, none of the other hospitals will either. Tomorrow has to go off without a hitch."

"Casey, buddy, you're making a mountain out of a molehill," he said, tilting his head to smile into her eyes. "Bell thinks you're great. The kids think you're great. And I . . ." His voice grew very husky as he sought her lips. "I think you'll set the world on fire."

Casey kept repeating Dare's words over and over like a mantra as she watched the four excited, wheelchair-bound children enter the riding ring. They were accompanied by eight adults—some parents, others volunteers who had come to help—and Dr. Bell, who was not looking the least bit impressed. The children's laughter died when they caught sight of the big, red horses, saddled and tied to the fence. The parents looked at the pawing, high-strung horses, then back at their children, and Casey could see the concern and, in some cases, fear in their eyes.

Would the program fizzle before it even had a chance to get off the ground? Darn it, she wished she had more experience. Should she push the children? Should she take things slow and easy?

Dare, sitting inside the door of the stables, realized immediately what was happening and what needed to be done. No way was he going to let Casey's program go down the drain without giving it everything he had. Collecting his saddle and bridle, he wheeled his chair outside, leading Rebel by the halter rope.

"Morning, y'all. Great day to go riding, isn't it?" he said while he swung his tack up on the fence, then tied Rebel. Rolling up to the nearest child, a girl of about ten with braces on her legs and pigtails in her black hair, he held out his hand. "Hi," he said, smiling at her. "My name's Dare. What's yours?"

She smiled back, self-conscious of the braces

on her teeth. "Lizabeth," she said shyly, almost in awe.

"What a pretty name for a very pretty girl."

And what a very special man, Casey thought as he introduced himself to Betty and Joe. His presence had a calming effect on the children, and the fact that he was in a wheelchair created an instant bond between them.

"And you're Billy Bob, aren't you?" Dare said as he approached the small, thin boy who was sitting apart from the rest of the group, completely ignoring the horses and the two women who had volunteered to come with him.

"How do you know me?" Billy Bob asked, looking at Dare out of the corner of his eye but ignoring his hand.

"I saw you when I was in the hospital," Dare said, backing off slightly to give the boy room.

"You were in my hospital?"

"Yep. When I first got hurt, but I couldn't stay." He swept his hand down his body. "You see, the beds were too short, and I was too long."

The children giggled at the thought of this giant sleeping in one of their beds, and Casey smiled, knowing the ice was truly broken.

"Well, now, I'm sure you want to meet the ponies," Dare said as he rolled his chair toward the Arabians. He moved from one horse to the next, patting its withers or rubbing an inquisitive nose as he introduced it. "As you can see they aren't afraid of a wheelchair, and they would love to take you for a ride. I bet you are wondering what's going to happen when you get on the horse. Well, if Casey would give me a hand, I'll show you."

Casey looked at Dare, her eyes wide in disbelief. Never in all her born days had she expected Dare to do this. To expose himself this way to so many people.

Don't do it, she wanted to tell him. The program isn't worth it. But he was already doing it—and would do more to make sure her dream came true.

"Casey, buddy. I'm sure the kids are getting anxious to ride their horses. Would you mind saddling Rebel for me?"

Spurred into action by his laughing words, she strode over to Rebel and began saddling him.

Dare rolled the wheelchair over to join her. "I want to tell you a bit about Rebel," he said, speaking more for the parents' and Bell's benefit than the children's. "He's a wild one. No one but me has ever ridden him. When I got hurt, I wondered if I'd be able to ride him again. Well, we've been working with him, and he's gotten used to me crawling in and out of his saddle. So have the other horses."

Dare shoved himself to his feet. Pain, sudden and crushing, gripped his back and thighs as his muscles went into spasms. His legs collapsed. He grabbed the saddle horn, his body sagging against the horse.

Casey sprang forward to help, so totally in tune

with Dare, she knew the moment the pain hit him. He warned her away with a slight shake of his head, then slowly, ever so slowly, began pulling his body up into the saddle.

Casey watched her proud, noble warrior haul himself into the saddle, and finally admitted the truth she'd been rejecting for weeks. She loved Dare. She had loved him all her life. For a few years she'd been sidetracked, trying so hard *not* to love him, she'd forgotten that loving Dare was as natural as breathing—and as vital to her well-being.

Finally he lifted his body high enough so his right leg flopped over the saddle. He straightened, shifted his weight, and before Casey could move to help him, he managed to shove his boots into the stirrups.

She looked up at him in delight. He was smiling at her—proudly, triumphantly. She smiled back, wishing she could shout for joy. Dare had moved his leg!

Turning Rebel around, he smiled down at the children. "There, you see, nothing to it. Thanks to Casey, I can ride Rebel again. With her help you'll be able to ride too."

Casey continued to look at Dare, her heart full of pride and joy and . . . love. How could she not love the man who was giving of himself so unselfishly, sacrificing his pride and his privacy so she could have her dream?

"Casey, buddy. Maybe you should tell everyone what you want them to do."

His soft voice nudged her into action, and she began talking to the children as she moved toward Sunshine. "We won't make you crawl onto the horses, kids. That's why we brought your parents along. One will hold the horse's head while the other will lift you into the saddle." Untying Sunshine, she led the horse over to the waiting children. "Now, who wants to ride Sunshine? Lizabeth?"

Dare sat on Rebel, watching as Casey worked with the children and their parents, feeling so proud of her, he thought he would burst. She had so much positive energy that people felt good being around her. Even Dr. Bell was looking impressed, Dare noticed, and gave Casey a slow wink and a thumbs-up the next time she glanced his way.

Soon all the children, except Billy Bob, were in the saddle, and the parents were leading the horses around the ring.

"I don't want to go," Billy Bob said, stubbornly shaking his head.

"The poor kid's afraid," one of the volunteers said, looking distressed. "Maybe we shouldn't force him."

Billy Bob thrust out his chin. "I am not afraid."

"Maybe you'd like to come up in front of me for the first time," Dare suggested quietly, leaning forward in the saddle to smile down at the towheaded boy.

Billy Bob tilted back his head and looked at Dare in surprise. "You're the only man who's ever rode Rebel."

"Yeah, but I figure you're brave enough to ride him. Would you like Casey to lift you aboard?"

For a moment the boy hesitated, then held out his arms to Casey. "Okay."

Casey lifted him up to Dare, then fussed a bit, moving Billy Bob's legs into a comfortable position. She stood with one hand on the boy's leg, one hand on Dare's muscular thigh, looking up at them. This was the first time she'd ever seen Billy Bob excited or even interested in anything, and it was all because of Dare, Casey thought. He was so good with children. He'd make a terrific father.

Dare deserved to have children of his own. And a wife who didn't live with the constant fear that she might pop a blood vessel and die, or worse—live and not be able to love him. With a soft sigh, she turned and walked away.

Dare watched Casey go, wondering why she was looking deflated all of a sudden. It was no wonder she was strung out. She had a hell of a lot of responsibility riding on her shoulders, he thought, then he turned his attention to Billy Bob. The boy was so thin, he barely weighed more than his artificial legs, and as they rode around the ring Dare felt a longing to put some meat on Billy Bob's bones and some happiness back into his life.

Casey had told him that the car crash, which had robbed Billy Bob of his legs, had also killed his parents. What was going to happen to the boy when he finally learned to walk again?

Three hours later Dare was still wishing he could do something special for Billy Bob. They had finished eating hamburgers, which he had cooked on the barbecue, and Billy Bob had crawled onto his lap to eat a piece of Casey's super duper Chocolate-Chip-Chocolate cake. He was probably spoiling the kid, Dare knew, but Billy Bob had no one to spoil him.

"So, do you want to be a cowboy when you grow up?" Dare asked the boy.

"You kiddin', mister?" Billy Bob licked the chocolate icing off his fingers. "A cowboy has to ride good. I ain't been in the saddle before."

"Well, you did a good job today. With a bit more practice you'll be riding the range soon."

"You really think so?"

"Sure do, partner."

"Are you going to ride the range too?"

"You bet."

"When?"

Dare chuckled at Billy Bob's persistence. Deciding it might help if he set a good example, Dare told him, "I'll ride over to the Regent Ranch tomorrow and ask them if I can hire on."

"King. That's who you are." Mr. Tompkins, Lizabeth's father, strolled over to stand beside Dare's chair. "You're one of the King brothers, aren't you? *The Daredevil.* The one who fights oil-well fires."

"Yeah."

"Well, how about that? What happened to you? Why are you in a wheelchair? I hope it isn't permanent."

"It isn't," Casey said as she moved to Dare's side. "He'll be on his feet in no time."

"So you've been helping him walk again. Isn't that marvelous." Mrs. Tompkins gushed, making Casey's hair bristle even more. She was definitely going to take the woman aside before she left and impress upon her about the importance of keeping Dare's injury a secret.

"What is marvelous is the program Casey is planning for the children," Dare said, smiling at Casey, thinking she was doing it again, protecting him. Lord, how he loved this wonderful woman. "Why don't you tell them about it, Casey."

Casey moved away from Dare and began talking, hoping to distract everyone's attention from him. She succeeded—except for herself. As she fielded questions from the excited parents her gaze kept going back to Dare. Head bowed, he was talking quietly to Billy Bob and even coaxed a smile from the boy.

Then he did something that made her want to cry. Somehow he managed to convince Billy Bob to stand on his feet and push Dare's wheelchair.

The memory of the triumph on the little boy's face stayed with Casey for the rest of the day, while she helped load the children into the van for the ride back to the hospital, while she joined Dare in the stable and silently helped him finish brushing the horses. But later that night, as she lay with his head cradled against her breasts, she finally gave voice to her thoughts.

"Thank you, Dare, for what you did today," she said, knowing she'd never be able to thank him enough for making her program a success. He had sacrificed his pride, had shown everyone how vulnerable he was, all because of her.

He nuzzled her soft, plump breast, then smiled as he heard her heart tap a quick response. "I didn't do much. You did all the hard work."

"You were the shining star who led the way. If you hadn't come forward to show the children how tame the horses were, it could have been a disaster. Thanks to you, the children can hardly wait to come back. And Dr. Bell seemed to be impressed."

"He was. He told me you had a real winner and that he'd be backing you to the hilt," Dare said, trying to keep his voice light and easy. Even if his life depended on it, he'd never tell Casey what else Bell had said to him after he'd finished his quick but thorough examination. *You're making some progress, King, but don't get your hopes up. You're not about to walk anytime soon.*

"He told me too. Didn't you hear my whoop of joy?" Dare's chuckle was smothered as she hugged him close. "But what really touched my heart was when you got Billy Bob to walk. How did you manage it? We've been trying for months."

"It's simple," he said softly. "I asked him to do something for me. To push my chair."

Do something for Casey. Do something for others. That was the creed Dare followed, Casey thought, no matter what the cost.

"Are you really going to ride over to the ranch tomorrow?" she asked when she finally managed to control the urge to tell him how much she loved him. The best thing she could do for Dare was to get out of his life as soon as he no longer needed her. She could never make him as happy as he deserved to be.

"I thought I'd call the Baron and see if he wanted to go for a ride. It would do him good to get up on a horse again."

"Darrick King, you are one very special man," Casey said, her heart overflowing with love. Once again Dare was reaching out to someone else. Once again it took all her control not to tell him she loved him.

"You got that wrong, darlin'," he drawled huskily as he kissed her turgid nipple. "You're the special person in these here parts."

"Well, would you do something for me?" she asked breathlessly.

"Anything, darlin'."

Would you tell me you love me? The words almost leaped from the tip of her tongue. Just in time she held them back. What right did she have to ask for

Dare's love when she didn't have the courage to love him completely?

"Would you make love to me," she whispered instead.

"Gladly."

But even as he loved her Dare wondered what he had to do to win her trust. How could he convince Casey that he would never leave her? Much later, as he lay awake holding her while she slept, he realized that there was nothing he could do to *win* her trust. Casey would have to *give* her trust to him.

In the early-morning hours he wakened to the sound of the mockingbird and realized there was something else he could do. He could tell Casey that he loved her. He'd wait, though, until he could walk again. Despite what Bell had said, he *was* going to walk again. Soon. Very soon.

Dare still hadn't returned from the Regent Ranch by the time Casey arrived home from the hospital at noon. When a truck pulled into the driveway, she rushed to the front door, wondering if something had happened to him.

Laramie Jones stepped out of the cab and ran lightly up the steps as Casey opened the door wide.

"Laramie, it's great to see you," Casey greeted the tall, lanky foreman of the Boone Blowout Control Company. "Did you just get back from Colombia?"

"This morning. King put out the word he wanted this." Laramie held up a large red tin box. "So I brought it out to him."

"He isn't here, but come on in and have a cup of coffee," Casey offered, thinking Laramie looked as if he needed it. His golden eyes were red-rimmed, his craggy features lined with fatigue.

He followed her into the kitchen, placed the box on the table, pulled out a chair, and dropped wearily into it. Removing his Stetson, he rifled his long fingers through his shaggy hair, then settled the hat on the back of his head.

Casey set a mug of coffee and piece of leftover chocolate cake in front of Laramie, then sat down opposite him, looking at the scratched and battered tin box as she sipped her own coffee. "What's in it?"

"Don't have a clue, but King has been carting it around ever since I've known him." Laramie forked a piece of cake into his mouth and "hmm-med" his appreciation. "I remember once he went back to get it—through a hail of rebel bullets while the rest of us waited in the chopper." He pointed to a rusty crease on the side of the tin. "That's how close the bullets came to hitting him."

Casey gasped in dismay. "He's crazy! He has always been a daredevil."

"No, Casey, he hasn't. He's the one of the most cautious men I've ever known. That's why the boys would follow him—have followed him—into hell and back." Laramie finished the cake and washed it down with a gulp of coffee. "Where is he?"

"Over at the Regent Ranch, riding with his father."

"He's riding!" Laramie shot her a quick smile. "Hey, that's great news. So that means he's walking too?"

"No, he isn't," she said, then hastened to reassure him. "But he will as soon as he learns to manage his crutches."

"Dammit all, he shouldn't have been hurt. Just like Cas shouldn't have been killed." Laramie looked down at his hands. "I'm real sorry about your father, Casey. The boys and me . . . well, we felt sick about it."

"Thanks." Rising abruptly, she walked over to the counter to retrieve the coffeepot.

"King was pretty tore up too," Laramie continued softly. "It was the only time I've seen him lose his cool. First he frightened that reporter, Billings, so badly that the man wet his pants—and King didn't even touch him. When we arrived at the well, Dare smashed up the inside of the construction trailer with his bare hands."

The thought that Dare had been hurting so badly was staggering. She now knew the reason for the scars on his hand, but she wondered if the wounds in his soul would ever heal.

"And then he got mad," Laramie continued as Casey silently filled his mug. "Swore he'd kill that fire if it was the last thing he did. It almost did get him, you know."

She collapsed onto the chair, her legs no longer willing to hold her. "No, I didn't know."

"Afterward, he was real quiet. I stuck to him like a sweaty shirt for days, but I learned real quick he wasn't about to do anything foolish. He's different now. The fun has gone out of taming wells. I think he's been wanting to come home and run the ranch."

Maybe she had been mistaken, Casey thought as she digested Laramie's words. Maybe Dare wasn't like her father, after all. Maybe he didn't want to chase wild wells for the rest of his life. "Then why hasn't he quit?"

"Because he needs the money to pay off—" Laramie clamped his mouth shut, pulled his Stetson down over his eyes.

Casey frowned at him. Something was wrong. She'd had the feeling before, at the christening party, and had ignored it, afraid of what she would learn. "What does Dare need money for?" she asked finally.

"I . . . I—" The beeper on his belt sounded. Laramie shot out of his chair and headed for the phone.

Deep in thought, Casey barely heard Laramie's responses but knew subconsciously he'd be chasing another blowout. He confirmed it a moment later when he hung up the receiver and made a beeline for the door.

"Got a bad one in New Mexico. Tell King to get better real quick. We need him." Then he was gone.

Casey stared at his retreating back and came to a decision. It was way past time she found out the truth about the Boone Blowout Control Company. And what better time than now, when everyone would be in an uproar.

ELEVEN

Where was Casey? Dare wondered, disappointed she hadn't come down to the stables when he'd ridden in. He planted his homemade crutches firmly on the ground and swung his body up the path toward the house. Like a kid with a new toy, he wanted to show off; let her see how well he could walk. Not that he could call his "plunk-swing-thump motion" walking, but it was a start. And if things went well, he'd soon be walking Casey down the aisle.

Today, when he'd gotten off Rebel to help his father build a rose trellis for Madre, he'd realized why he'd been having so much trouble using the hospital crutches; he hadn't trusted them to hold his weight.

The distrust was the result of too many years of depending on his own equipment—which he'd often built himself or had at least checked and rechecked until he knew exactly what it would do in any given situation. A caution that had kept his men alive, but that was also difficult to overcome.

The old hickory limbs he'd found out behind the barn wouldn't break—and he'd fashioned a set of crutches, crude but effective. When he'd walked into the rose garden, the Baron had almost lost his legendary cool. Madre had cried, but then Madre had been feeling a bit weepy anyway, because the Baron had offered to build the trellis she'd wanted for years.

All in all, it had been a good day, and he could hardly wait to share it with Casey. Where was she? he wondered again as he entered the house and found it empty.

Halfway across the kitchen floor, he spied the battered tin box on the table and quickly thumped his way over to it. The crutches clattered to the floor as he opened the lid.

Discovering that everything was safe, he replaced the lid, sat down, crossed his arms over the box, and bowed his head on his bent wrists. Long minutes later he lifted his head, reached for the phone, and punched in the office number.

"Is Laramie there?" he asked Maureen.

"Thanks, big boy, I just won my bet," Maureen said, relief overlaying the banter in her voice. "He's on the other line, but I'll put him on."

"King, how are you?" Laramie asked a moment later. "Sorry I missed you earlier."

"Why didn't you hang around?"

"Got a call about a fire in New Mexico."

"Bad?"

"Yeah."

"Anyone hurt?"

"No, but it has the makings of a killer. And Hopper has just had a blowout in West Texas."

"Did you turn him down?"

"He's on hold."

If they could kill these two wells, Dare thought, and if everything went off without a hitch, he could quit, or at least slow down. Laramie was ready to take over, and he was ready to hand things over to his foreman as soon as he got out from under the debt. "Tell Hopper we'll do it, then send out the chopper for me," he told Laramie. "I'll kill it while you take care of the one in New Mexico."

"Casey isn't going to like this, King." Laramie cleared his throat. "And I gotta warn you, you're not one of her favorite people right now."

"What's up?"

"I'm afraid I spilled the beans while I was out at the ranch. She blew into the office like a tornado, tore us apart, then stormed out again."

Dare cursed softly, succinctly. "Get the chopper in the air, Laramie. I'll definitely need rescuing when she hits here."

"Will do. And, King, I'm sorry."

So was he, Dare thought as he retrieved his crutches and headed for the bedroom to pack. He had hoped Casey would never learn the truth.

When her Jeep screeched up to the house twenty minutes later, Dare was back in the kitchen, sitting in the wheelchair he'd wheeled up from the stables, his crutches propped alongside his bag at the front door.

She strode through the kitchen door, then stopped in the middle of the room. "I've spent an interesting afternoon talking to people," she said, pointing her forefinger at him in accusation. "Your lawyer and accountant to name two, after I'd been to the land-titles office."

"Now, Casey, buddy, don't get your tail in a knot." He raised his hand, palm up, and tried a coaxing smile. She glared at him.

"How long were you going to continue this charade, Dare, old buddy? How long did you think you could hide the fact you've been bailing Dad out of trouble for years?"

He started to push himself to his feet. "Casey—"

"Sit down. I have a bone to pick with you, and I don't want to be distracted because I'm afraid you might fall."

Dare sank back into the chair, realizing how upset Casey was; she would never deliberately say anything to hurt him. "Would you let me explain," he asked quietly, "or do you want to rant awhile?"

"What is there to explain? All I have, I owe to you. You put me through college."

"Only because Cas didn't have much money after he paid your mother's medical expenses."

She stood with hands on her hips, her body trembling with suppressed emotion. "You know and I know that Dad never had any money because he gambled—on horses, dogs, ball games, cards. You name it; he played it. Badly." She pointed a shaking finger at Dare. "He even lost his share of the company in a poker game before he died, didn't he? You had to take out a loan to buy it back, didn't you?"

"Case—"

"For the last three years the company has been paying me handsome dividends . . . which I've been spending on horses. And you—" Her voice broke and she drew in a sharp breath. "You've been working your butt off because you're up to your ears in debt. That's why you've continued to work when you've been wanting to quit. That's the reason you can't walk."

"Case—"

"It's all my fault. All along you've been fighting those horrible fires, doing those dangerous things because you were *taking care* of me."

"Please, princess. Please don't beat yourself up over this," he said, shoving himself to his feet. He held out his hand, but she turned away. He took a step toward her, lost his balance, then fell with a clang back into his chair.

She swung around and stared at him, her fingers pressed to her lips, her eyes bright with concern. Lowering her hands, she wrapped her arms around her waist. "And I own this ranch because of you," she said after a moment. "You were the old geezer from California. You bought it when Mama got so sick at the end, and Dad desperately wanted to buy her a condo before she died. Why didn't you tell me what was going on?"

"Because I didn't want to hurt your father's pride. I offered him a loan, but he refused it. He had always planned to buy back the ranch and give it to you."

"So when he died, you gave it to me *in his name.*" Crossing the distance between them, she placed her hand on his shoulder. "Because of you, I have everything I dare to dream for," she said, gazing into his eyes. "The home I love. My horses. And a chance to do something special for the children. All my life I have taken gifts from you, Dare, but I can't go on taking. This is too much."

"Gifts! Casey, darlin', I was being selfish." He captured her hand and held it gently, afraid that if he held it as tightly as he wanted, she would pull away. "Sure I paid off your father's gambling debts because I didn't want to take the chance of losing the company. As for your owning half of the company—you would have owned it anyway, if we'd gotten married. I bought this ranch because I dreamed of one day living here with you. It would have been yours too."

"Well, we didn't get married. I left you standing at the altar. And I can't take the ranch from you."

"The ranch is a gift. I gave it to you because—"

Pulling her hand out of his grasp, she abruptly turned away. "I can't accept your gift. You'll have to take it back."

He caught her arm and stopped her. "Where are you going?"

"To the springs."

"This time I won't be coming after you, Casey, so please hear me out before you go."

She half turned, stared pointedly at her arm. Releasing it, he picked up the tin box.

"If you insist on giving me back the ranch," he continued softly, "I'll have to return the gifts you've given me."

"My gifts?"

"Yes, these." Lifting the lid, he removed a gold-covered scrapbook and handed it to her. "Your hearts."

She took the scrapbook and flipped through the pages, staring in stunned disbelief at the hearts she'd made and given to Dare over the years. "You kept these?"

"Yes, Casey, I kept them. All of them. Take a good look before you decide if you want them back. And while you're making up your mind, my darlin', please remember one thing. These are the most precious gifts I have ever received . . . except when you gave yourself to me."

Suddenly Casey couldn't stand to be in the same room with Dare any longer. Bolting through the door, she ran down to the stables. Moments later she was riding Sundancer bareback across the field to the springs, the scrapbook clutched under her arm.

She tried to look at the scrapbook, but her vision blurred, and she bowed her head, overcome by memories. This time the springs held no comfort. This time Dare wasn't there to hold her and talk to her, to help her face her fears. This time she would have to do it herself.

One by one she took out the memories and confronted them. The guilt, anger, and love she had felt for the three most important people in her life—her mother, father, and Dare. And the fear that had haunted her all her life—the fear of being abandoned by the people she loved. The emotions were all interwoven so tightly, it was difficult to sort them out, but slowly she did . . . because overriding everything else was the knowledge that Dare had always been there for her. Dare would never desert her.

Gradually her vision cleared enough to look at the scrapbook he had so carefully, lovingly made. Each heart was mounted on a separate page, which was labeled with the date, occasion, and Casey's age. These were his most precious treasures. How could she ever take them from him?

Flipping to the beginning of the book, she gazed at the first heart she'd made him when she was five. She opened it, read the words she'd laboriously copied inside:

I give you my heart. I know you will keep it safe.

And Dare had kept it safe. He'd been fourteen years old. The age when most boys would have thoughtlessly torn up the heart or quickly lost it. Dare had placed it carefully into a scrapbook and had kept it safe. Not only the first heart, but all the others she'd given him.

How could she have been so smart when she was five, and so dumb when she was twenty-two? Casey thought in dismay. He'd given her the Princess when she was one, an education, and a home . . . and most recently had helped her do "something special" for her special children.

He had given her more, Casey realized as a sense of peace seeped into her soul. He had given her the courage to dream again. Rising to her feet, she swung onto Sundancer's back, anxious to share her dream with Dare.

But when she entered the kitchen a few minutes later and found his note on the table, she realized it might be too late.

Casey was standing at the altar, a vision of loveliness in her wedding gown and veil. She was waiting for him, Dare knew, but he couldn't go to her. He couldn't walk.

She turned and gazed expectantly down the aisle, her hand stretched out to him. All the wedding guests turned and looked at him, too, their eyes full of pity. He tried to take a step toward her, but his leg wouldn't move. He tried again and fell—

Dare woke with a start, his heart pounding, and found himself lying on a cot in the construction trailer. The trailer was shaking, and outside, the raging well was roaring louder than the blast furnaces of hell. He'd fallen all right, Dare remembered—flat on his back in the mud and the oil when his crutches had slipped. Curly and Bill had hauled him into the trailer, then had left him—cursing on the cot—taking his crutches with them. Somewhere in the middle of calling them a couple of mule-headed jackasses, he'd dozed off into the first sleep he'd had since he'd arrived on the site two days before.

He sat up, raked a dirty hand through his sweat-caked hair, then wiped it down over his gritty, bloodshot eyes.

Thank God his men were loyal. Thank God he'd placed guards on the gate to keep out the press. Thank God the oil patch still didn't know he couldn't walk. If he could pull off this job—on crutches—maybe the fallout wouldn't be too bad when everyone learned about his accident. Maybe he would still have a company when this was all over.

The noise level increased as the trailer door opened. Dare lifted his head, ready to apologize to the men. The words died as Casey entered the room. She was wearing jeans, a denim shirt, and a yellow hard hat, and was clutching the tin box under her arm. She was the most welcome sight he'd ever seen.

Hands gripping his knees, he stared at her, hardly daring to believe his eyes. Casey had come to see him—at a wild well.

"Casey, you came." Swallowing the lump in his throat, he continued hoarsely, "I was so afraid I'd lost you." He held out his arms and she flew into them, the tin box dropping onto the cot, her hard hat falling to the floor. Settling her onto his knee, he held her tightly, rocking her back and forth for a few moments before releasing her slightly to gaze into her eyes.

Her gaze caressed him as she brushed a trembling hand across his whiskered cheek. "Oh, Dare. Are you all right?"

"I'm fine." He gave her a reassuring smile. "Just a bit bleary-eyed from lack of sleep and filthy from wallowing around in the mud. And now I've got you filthy too."

"It doesn't matter." She hugged him tightly, pressing herself against his chest. "As long as you're safe."

He rocked her again, wishing the well was capped so she wouldn't have to worry about him anymore. "What are you doing here, princess?" he asked after a while. "This is the last place in the world I ever expected to see you."

Reluctantly she unwrapped her arms, slid off his knee onto the cot, groped for and found the tin box. "I came to bring these back where they belong," she said, handing him the box. "In your safe keeping."

He looked at the box, then up at her, his eyes full of hope. "Does this mean you'll keep the ranch?" he asked as he placed the box on the cot.

She drew in a deep breath and released it slowly, her wide eyes never leaving his. "On condition that you'll live there with me. I know you don't love me but—"

"Casey, I love you," he said, reaching out to take both her hands in his. "I have always loved you."

"You do?" she asked, her eyes growing even wider.

"I know I've never told you, but I thought you knew."

"I thought you felt you had to look after me."

She looked so stunned, it was all Dare could do to keep from taking her into his arms and kissing her until her last doubt was gone. But this time he had to do more than kiss her, he decided. This time she needed to hear the words. "Maybe I felt that way when you were a child, but everything changed the day you turned sixteen—the day I first kissed you," he said, his eyes growing soft with memories. "For the next two years I tried to keep my feelings under control, tried to tell myself that you would be better off marrying someone closer to your own age." She started to object, but he stopped her with a shake of his head. "The summer you spent with us in the oil patch was pure hell, and when you stepped off the plane in Edmonton the following Christmas, I knew I wanted to marry you."

"Why then?" she asked, still looking bewildered.

Raising her hand to his lips, he brushed a kiss across her knuckles then lowered her hand again, soothing the spot he'd kissed with the callused pad of his thumb. "Because you were generous enough to leave the warm, sunny south to fly up to the frigid north because you thought I shouldn't be alone for Christmas."

"But I don't understand," she said, shaking her head as she remembered the occasion. "You put me up in the best hotel. You bought me a beautiful dress because I hadn't brought one with me. You wined and dined me, and when you danced with me I thought I was the luckiest woman in the world to be in your arms. I would have spent the rest of the night in your arms, if you had asked."

He laughed softly. "Believe me, I knew exactly how you were feeling. Especially after you told me you were thinking of quitting college so you could stay with me. Leaving you at the door to your room that night was the hardest thing I'd ever done."

"Then why didn't you at least tell me you loved me?" she cried out.

"Because I didn't think it was fair to you, Casey. You had almost four years of college ahead of you. I wanted you to date, to have fun, to do all the things you missed when you were looking after your mother. I didn't want you to feel tied down to me."

"So, you decided what was best for me. You gave me no chance to choose. I would have finished college, Dare, but I would have also married you, then and there. You didn't give me a chance to prove to you that I was grown up." She paused, took a deep breath, then smiled at him. "Well, I have finally grown up completely. Will you marry me?"

"Oh, Casey, darlin'." He gazed at her, his eyes dark with love, then swept her into his arms again, hugging her close, pressing her head against his chest. "I want to marry you, princess, more than anything else in the world," he said softly into her ear. "I want to spend the rest of my life loving you, and cherishing you, and living with you on your ranch—"

"Our ranch," she said, her voice muffled against his chest.

He chuckled and released her slightly so she could breathe. "Our ranch. I've been thinking about it a lot these last two days. Maybe Billy Bob could come and live with us. Maybe we could adopt him. Maybe we could even adopt a few more kids like him. Lord knows, we have enough bedrooms."

She hugged him. "Oh, Dare, what a super, super idea. It would really make all my dreams come true."

"Then hold on to your dreams for a little while longer, Casey. Until I can walk again."

Lifting her head, she stared at him in confusion. "Walk again?"

"When we get married, Casey, I want to walk with you up the aisle."

She looked at the wheelchair, sitting at the foot of the cot, then back at him. "What if you can never walk again?" she asked, her throat so tight, she could barely speak. "What if you have to use a wheelchair or crutches for the rest of your life?"

He gazed at her, hesitated, then shook his head. "I . . . don't know."

Abruptly she pulled out of his arms. "Now let me see if I have this straight. You'll only marry me if you can walk?"

"I don't want to be a burden on you for the rest of your life, Casey," he said, wanting to put his arms around her again but afraid to touch her for fear he'd lose what little remained of his self-control. "You had to look after your mother when you were growing up, and now you're talking about looking after children who will also need special care. I want to be able to help you with them, not be an extra burden on you."

"I love you, Dare, and I want to marry you. Now!" she said stubbornly, fighting for her happiness, knowing that if she didn't he might bow completely out of her life.

"But it's not fair to you, Casey. I can't do it."

"Because you're still trying to protect me. You still don't think I've grown up."

"That's not true, Casey."

"Oh, but it is. You still don't think I love you the way a woman loves a man. Well, let me tell you how much I love you, Darrick King. I love you so much that I want to marry you, even if you continue to fight wild wells for the rest of your life, because I would rather have a few years, or months, or hours of being your wife—if that is all the time we are granted together—than not have you in my life at all."

"Casey," he said, then paused as the rest of his words got stuck in his throat.

Pressing her fingers against his lips, she continued, "I love you so much, Dare, that I am willing to have your children."

He swallowed hard. "Casey, darlin', I told you I didn't want you to take the risk."

"Well, I'm willing to take the risk, Dare, but only if I'm married to you. Because you're the only man I trust. I know you'd never leave me if something happened to me."

She leaned forward, pressed a kiss against his warm, rough lips where a moment before her fingers had lingered, then she raised her head and looked at him, her eyes shining with love. "I love you enough to let you look after me, if necessary. Do you love me enough to let me look after you?"

He gazed at her for a dozen painful heartbeats, his eyes dark with yearning. "Casey, darlin', please give me a few more months. I know I'll be able to walk well enough by then."

She shook her head. "I've waited for years to marry you, King. I don't want to wait any longer." Reaching across his legs, she picked up the tin box and gave it to him. "Take a look at the new heart in the scrapbook, Dare. It's an invitation to our wedding. I'll be at the chapel a week from today, waiting for you at the altar."

Leaning forward, she kissed him, then without another word, she rose and walked out of the trailer.

Once again—at Casey's insistence—the organist began playing the wedding march on the stroke of two. In the vestibule the two bridesmaids, dressed in floating blue georgette, paused in the arched doorway and looked into the small chapel which was filled with flowers and people.

"He's not there," Marnie whispered anxiously as she turned back to Casey, who was standing in the middle of the vestibule, wearing her grandmother's wedding dress and veil and holding a bouquet of red roses.

"Duke and Dev are waiting, but Dare hasn't arrived yet," Kristi said, peering over Marnie's shoulder. She also turned to Casey. "Are you sure you want us to go ahead?"

"Yes, yes, don't worry," Casey said, smiling at the two women. "Dare will come."

Heart pounding, Casey watched as first Marnie, then Kristi began walking down the aisle toward their husbands.

Dare would come, wouldn't he? He'd always come whenever she had needed him.

But this time it would serve her right if he left her standing at the altar, she thought as the ignominy she was asking Dare to face struck home. Dare was such a shy, proud man, and once again she was asking him to sacrifice his pride—this time to appear before his family and friends in a wheelchair.

Why hadn't she waited a little while longer until he had at least learned to use crutches? He had waited so long for her.

She took a deep breath, wishing she could call off the wedding, wishing she could go to him and beg him for forgiveness.

Behind her, the outside door opened. She turned and watched, with her hand clutched against her breast, as Dare, dressed in the Spanish wedding clothes he'd worn before, walked into the vestibule on crutches.

"Dare, you came," she said, her voice velvet soft with joy.

"Did you think I would desert you?"

"Never. Not in a million years."

He smiled then, his slow, sexy smile that made her knees tremble so badly that her skirt began to shake. She stepped closer and caught hold of his arm, smiling at him through her lace veil. "And you're on crutches!" she said, barely able to believe her eyes. Her handsome hero was *standing* there before her.

"I couldn't let you walk down the aisle by yourself, princess," he said softly as he lifted her veil. Then he kissed her, trying to tell her how much he loved her with his lips because he wasn't much good with words. Trying to tell her that he would walk through hell—had walked through hell—to be at her side today. Vowing to tell her as soon as the ceremony was over that she wouldn't have to worry about him fighting another wild well again.

Behind him, Laramie cleared his voice. "King, the music's stopped."

Reluctantly Dare raised his head and gazed at Casey, his eyes caressing her face. "Lord, you're beautiful," he said as he bent toward her again.

"Watch it, King. We're late enough already," Laramie warned, then smiled at Casey. "Sorry, I couldn't get him here earlier, honey. First—"

"Later," Dare said, handing Laramie his crutches, his eyes never leaving Casey's. He held out his arm to her. "Shall we go, my darlin'."

"Dare! You . . . you can walk?" she whispered, so surprised and elated that she could hardly speak.

"If I can lean on you, buddy, I figure I'm good for a oneway trip down the aisle."

Placing her hand in the crook of his arm, she smiled up at him. "Yes, Dare, you can lean on me. Isn't that what buddies are for?"

Together they stepped into the chapel and paused as a murmur of relief swept through the guests who had been standing, anxiously watching the door. The organist began playing again, and Casey and Dare—still gazing steadfastly into each other's eyes—began walking down the aisle.

Dare walked slowly, haltingly, each step a major victory, the next one a potential defeat. Casey could feel the tension in his ramrod-straight body. She could also feel his pain and the effort he was making to place one foot in front of the other. But he was smiling at her with his wide, wonderful smile, making her feel as if she was the most beautiful woman in the world. Making her feel very, very lucky to be the *Daredevil*'s woman.

She heard someone sob and glanced at the guests, noting with surprise that most of them were crying. Flashing them a quick smile of reassurance, she turned her eyes once more to Dare, feeling so proud of him, she wanted to cry and laugh and sing. Feeling as if the sun would always rise and set on him. Knowing he would always be her buddy . . . her lover . . . her king.

Finally they reached the altar where the minister was waiting, along with the entire King family—Kristi and Dev, Marnie and Duke, Madre and the Baron, and the Duchess, holding little David. Casey smiled at each of them, silently thanking them for being her family, then she smiled once more at Dare, who had always been at the center of her life—and would always be.

"Dearly beloved, we are gathered here together," the minister began, and continued to read the familiar words of the wedding ceremony . . . until it came time for the couple to repeat the vows.

Then Dare spoke up, knowing that all he had to say was "I do" but wanting to tell Casey what was really in his heart.

"I, Darrick King, have always loved you, Casey Amelia Boone, and I promise to love you, forever," he began softly, gazing tenderly into her eyes.

Yes, Dare had always loved her, Casey thought, smiling at him, her green eyes never leaving his. From the day she was born, she'd been blessed by his love.

"And I promise to always look after you, Casey Amelia Boone, to cherish you in sickness and in health for as long as we both shall live."

And he would do just that, Casey knew, believing in the depths of her heart that if something did happen to her, Dare would look after her. He would cherish her always.

"But more than that, my darlin', I promise to let you cherish me in sickness as well as in health, for as long as we both shall live," he said. His expression was still solemn, but his eyes were smiling down at her.

Casey laughed softly, then gave a prayer of thanks. She would always have trouble getting this tough Texan to let her do anything for him, but from now on she'd remind him of his vow. To think that Dare, this very shy, very private man, would be saying these beautiful, heartfelt words to her! She started to speak, but he shook his head, and she realized there was even more he wanted to say.

"I also promise you, Casey Amelia Boone, that I will never leave you. I will stay by your side, loving you, for as long as I shall live."

He paused, and she stared at him, so overcome by the special significance of his words that she could barely breathe. How had she ever thought that this warm, wonderful man would leave her? Dare would always be there beside her, and her life would be fuller, richer, more meaningful because he gave her the courage to dream.

"And when the time comes for me to draw my last breath in this world, I will still not leave you," he said, his voice softer, deeper, but clear enough to reach to the very back of the chapel and into everyone's heart.

Raising his hand, he laid it tenderly against her cheek, making her feel so cherished, so adored.

"Whenever you feel the warm, west wind on your face, my darlin', it will be my hand touching you."

Gently he stroked the tender skin beneath her ear, making her feel as if she were his precious princess, and that he would always keep her safe.

"When you hear the mockingbird greeting the dawn, it will be my voice calling to you, and I will stay with you all the day long."

Then he smiled at her, the smile that had always made her feel so special . . . so beloved, and she smiled back, her green eyes shining with gold.

"When darkness falls and the moonlight steals through your bedroom window, it will be me lying beside you, loving you."

Casey gazed into Dare's eyes, loving him so much that it filled her heart and soul and every fiber of her being. And his next words made her realize that her love would never end.

Leaning over, he whispered the rest of his vow against her lips, "And when the time comes for you to leave this world, my darlin', I will still be by your side . . . loving you throughout eternity."

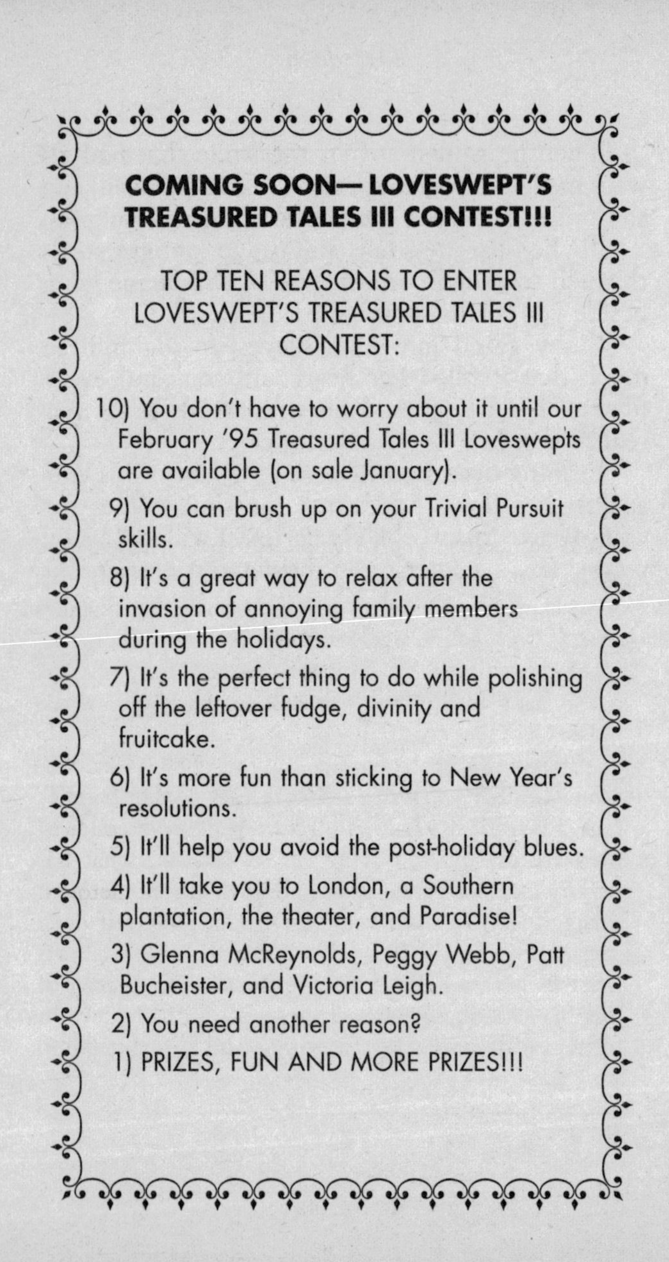
COMING SOON— LOVESWEPT'S TREASURED TALES III CONTEST!!!
TOP TEN REASONS TO ENTER LOVESWEPT'S TREASURED TALES III CONTEST:
10) You don't have to worry about it until our February '95 Treasured Tales III Loveswepts are available (on sale January).
9) You can brush up on your Trivial Pursuit skills.
8) It's a great way to relax after the invasion of annoying family members during the holidays.
7) It's the perfect thing to do while polishing off the leftover fudge, divinity and fruitcake.
6) It's more fun than sticking to New Year's resolutions.
5) It'll help you avoid the post-holiday blues.
4) It'll take you to London, a Southern plantation, the theater, and Paradise!
3) Glenna McReynolds, Peggy Webb, Patt Bucheister, and Victoria Leigh.
2) You need another reason?
1) PRIZES, FUN AND MORE PRIZES!!!

THE EDITOR'S CORNER

What better way to celebrate the holidays than with four terrific new LOVESWEPTs! And this month we are excited to present you with romances that are full of passion, humor, and most of all, true love—everything that is best about this time of year. So sit back and indulge yourself in the magic of the season.

Starting things off is the fabulous Mary Kay McComas with **PASSING THROUGH MIDNIGHT**, LOVESWEPT #722. Gil Howlett believes all women are mysteries, but he *has* to discover what has driven Dorie Devries into hiding in his hometown! Struggling with old demons, Dorie wonders if deep sorrow ever heals, but Gil's tenderness slowly wins her trust. Now he must soothe the wounded spirit of this big-city doctor who challenges him to believe in forgotten dreams. Heartwarming and heartbreaking,

Mary Kay's novels weave a marvelous tapestry of emotions into stories you wish would never end.

The wonderfully talented Debra Dixon wants to introduce you to **DOC HOLIDAY**, LOVESWEPT #723. Drew Haywood needs an enchantress to help give his son a holiday to remember—and no one does Christmas better than Taylor Bishop! She can transform a house into a home that smells of gingerbread and sparkles with tinsel, and kissing her is like coming out of the cold. She's spent her whole life caring for others, but when sweet temptation beckons, this sexy family man must convince her to break all her rules. With poignant humor and sizzling sensuality, Debra has crafted an unforgettable story of the magic of Christmas.

The ever-popular Adrienne Staff returns with **SPELLBOUND**, LOVESWEPT #724. Edward Rockford sees her first in the shadows and senses the pretty artist somehow holds the key to his secrets—but when he enters Jamie Payton's loft, he is stunned to discover that her painting reveals what he's hidden from all the world. Haunted by ghosts from the past, Jamie yearns to share his sanctuary. But can his seductive sorcery set her free? Conjured of equal parts destiny and mystery, passion and emotion, Adrienne's stories capture the imagination and compel the heart to believe once more in a love for all time.

Last but never least is Susan Connell with **RINGS ON HER FINGERS**, LOVESWEPT #725. She really knows how to fill her Christmas stockings, Steve Stratton decides with admiration at first sight of the long-legged brunette dressed as a holiday elf! Gwen Mansfield feels her heart racing like a runaway sleigh when the gorgeous architect invites her to play under his tree—and vows to be good. A jinxed love life has made her wary, but maybe Steve is the one to change her luck. Susan Connell has always written about intrepid heroes and damsels in just enough distress to make life interesting, but now she delivers the perfect Christmas present, complete with surprises and glittering fun!

Happy reading!

With best wishes,

Beth de Guzman

Senior Editor

P.S. Don't miss the exciting women's novels that are coming your way from Bantam in January! **HEAVEN'S PRICE**, from blockbuster author Sandra Brown, is a classic romantic novel in hardcover for the first time; **LORD OF ENCHANTMENT,** by bestselling author Suzanne Robinson, is an enchanting tale of romance and intrigue on a stormy isle off the coast of Elizabethan England; **SURRENDER TO A STRANGER**, by Karyn Monk, is an utterly compelling, passionately romantic debut from an exceptionally talented new historical romance author. We'll be giving you a sneak peek at these terrific books in next month's LOVESWEPTs. And immediately following this page look for a preview of the exciting romances from Bantam that are *available now!*

ADAM'S FALL

by

"Ms. Brown's larger than life heroes and heroines make you believe all the warm, wonderful, wild things in life."
—*Rendezvous*

BLOCKBUSTER AUTHOR SANDRA BROWN—WHOSE NAME IS ALMOST SYNONYMOUS WITH *THE NEW YORK TIMES* BEST-SELLER LIST—OFFERS A CLASSIC ROMANTIC NOVEL THAT ACHES WITH EMOTION AND SIZZLES WITH PASSION. . . .

They still fought like cats and dogs, but their relationship drastically improved.

He still cursed her, accused her of being heartless out of pure meanness, and insisted that she pushed him beyond his threshold of pain and endurance.

She still cursed him and accused him of being a

gutless rich kid who, for the first time in his charmed life, was experiencing hardship.

He said she couldn't handle patients worth a damn.

She said he couldn't handle adversity worth a damn.

He said she taunted him unmercifully.

She said he whined incessantly.

And so it went. But things were definitely better.

He came to trust her just a little. He began to listen when she told him that he wasn't trying hard enough and should put more concentration into it. And he listened when she advised that he was trying too hard and needed to rest awhile.

"Didn't I tell you so?" She was standing at the foot of his bed, giving therapy to his ankle.

"I'm still not ready to tap dance."

"But you've got sensation."

"You stuck a straight pin into my big toe!"

"But you've got sensation." She stopped turning his foot and looked up toward the head of his bed, demanding that he agree.

"I've got sensation." The admission was grumbled, but he couldn't hide his pleased smile.

"In only two and a half weeks." She whistled. "You've come a long way, baby. I'm calling Honolulu today and ordering a set of parallel bars. You'll soon be able to stand between them."

His smile collapsed. "I'll never be able to do that."

"That's what you said about the wheelchair. Will you lighten up?"

"Will you?" He grunted with pain as she bent his knee back toward his chest.

"Not until you're walking."

"If you keep wearing those shorts, I'll soon be running. I'll be chasing you."

"Promises, promises."

"I thought I told you to dress more modestly."

"This is Hawaii, Cavanaugh. Everybody goes casual, or haven't you heard? I'm going to resist the movement now. Push against my hand. That's it. A little harder. Good."

"Ah, God," he gasped through clenched teeth. He followed her instructions, which took him through a routine to stretch his calf muscle. "The backs of your legs are sunburned," he observed as he put forth even greater effort.

"You noticed?"

"How could I help it? You flash them by me every chance you get. Think those legs of yours are long enough? They must start in your armpits. But how'd I get off on that? What were we talking about?"

"Why my legs were sunburned. Okay, Adam, let up a bit, then try it again. Come on now, no ugly faces. One more time." She picked up the asinine conversation in order to keep his mind off his discomfort. "My legs are sunburned because I fell asleep beside the pool yesterday afternoon."

"Is that what you're being paid an exorbitant amount of money to do? To nap beside my swimming pool?"

"Of course not!" After a strategic pause, she added, "I went swimming too." He gave her a baleful look and pressed his foot against the palm of her hand. "Good, Adam, good. Once more."

"You said that was the last one."
"I lied."
"You heartless bitch."
"You gutless preppy."
Things were swell.

"Susan Johnson brings sensuality to new heights and beyond."
—*Romantic Times*

Susan Johnson

NATIONALLY BESTSELLING AUTHOR OF *SEIZED BY LOVE* AND *OUTLAW*

PURE SIN

From the erotic imagination of bestselling author Susan Johnson comes a tale of exquisite pleasure that begins in the wilds of Montana—and ends in the untamed places of two lovers' hearts.

"A shame we didn't ever meet," Adam said with a seductive smile, his responses automatic with beautiful women. "Good conversation is rare."

She didn't suppose most women were interested exclusively in his conversation, Flora thought, as she took in the full splendor of his dark beauty and power. Even lounging in a chair, his legs casually crossed at the ankles, he presented an irresistible image of brute strength. And she'd heard enough rumor in the course of the evening to understand he enjoyed women—nonconversationally. "As rare as marital fidelity no doubt."

His brows rose fractionally. "No one's had the nerve to so bluntly allude to my marriage. Are you speaking of Isolde's or my infidelities?" His grin was boyish.

"Papa says you're French."

"Does that give me motive or excuse? And I'm only half French, as you no doubt know, so I may have less excuse than Isolde. She apparently prefers Baron Lacretelle's properties in Paris and Nice to my dwelling here."

"No heartbroken melancholy?"

He laughed. "Obviously you haven't met Isolde."

"Why did you marry then?"

He gazed at her for a moment over the rim of the goblet he'd raised to his lips. "You can't be that naive," he softly said, then quickly drained the glass.

"Forgive me. I'm sure it's none of my business."

"I'm sure it's not." The warmth had gone from his voice and his eyes. Remembering the reason he'd married Isolde always brought a sense of chaffing anger.

"I haven't felt so gauche in years," Flora said, her voice almost a whisper.

His black eyes held hers, their vital energy almost mesmerizing, then his look went shuttered and his grin reappeared. "How could you know, darling? About the idiosyncrasies of my marriage. Tell me now about your first sight of Hagia Sophia."

"It was early in the morning," she began, relieved he'd so graciously overlooked her faux pas. "The sun had just begun to appear over the crest of the—"

"Come dance with me," Adam abruptly said, leaning forward in his chair. "This waltz is a favorite of mine," he went on, as though they hadn't been discussing something completely different. Reaching over, he took her hands in his. "And I've been wanting to"—his hesitation was minute as he discarded the inappropriate verb—"hold you." He grinned. "You see how blandly circumspect my choice of words is." Rising, he gently pulled her to her feet. "Considering the newest scandal in my life, I'm on my best behavior tonight."

"But then scandals don't bother me." She was standing very close to him, her hands still twined in his.

His fine mouth, only inches away, was graced with a genial smile and touched with a small heated playfulness. "I thought they might not."

"When one travels as I do, one becomes inured to other people's notions of nicety." Her bare shoulders lifted briefly, ruffling the limpid lace on her décolletage. He noticed both the pale satin of her skin and the tantalizing swell of her bosom beneath the delicate lace. "If I worried about scandal," she murmured with a small smile, "I'd never set foot outside England."

"And you do."

"Oh yes," she whispered. And for a moment both were speaking of something quite different.

"You're not helping," he said in a very low voice. "I've sworn off women for the moment."

"To let your wounds heal?"

"Nothing so poetical." His quirked grin reminded her of a teasing young boy. "I'm reassessing my priorities."

"Did I arrive in Virginia City too late then?"

"Too late?" One dark brow arched infinitesimally.

"To take advantage of your former priorities."

He took a deep breath because he was already perversely aware of the closeness of her heated body, of the heady fragrance of her skin. "You're a bold young lady, Miss Bonham."

"I'm twenty-six years old, Mr. Serre, and independent."

"I'm not sure after marriage to Isolde that I'm interested in any more willful aristocratic ladies."

"Perhaps I could change your mind."

He thoughtfully gazed down at her, and then the faintest smile lifted the graceful curve of his mouth. "Perhaps you could."

"[Kay Hooper] writes with exceptional beauty and grace."
—*Romantic Times*

Kay Hooper

NATIONALLY BESTSELLING AUTHOR OF
THE WIZARD OF SEATTLE

ON WINGS OF MAGIC

One of today's most beloved romance authors, Kay Hooper captivates readers with the wit and sensuality of her work. Now the award-winning writer offers a passionate story filled with all the humor and tenderness her fans have come to expect—a story that explores the loneliness of heartbreak and the searing power of love. . . .

"Tell me, Kendall—why the charade?"

"Why not?" She looked at him wryly. "I am what people expect me to be."

"You mean men."

"Sure. Oh, I could rant and rave about not being valued for who I am instead of what I look like, but what good would that do? My way is much easier. And there's no harm done."

"I don't know about that." Seriously, he went on, "By being what people expect you to be, you don't give anyone the chance to see the real you."

Interested in spite of herself, she frowned thoughtfully. "But how many people really care what's beneath the surface, Hawke? Not many," she went on, answering her own question. "We all act out roles we've given ourselves, pretend to be things we're not—or things we want to be. And we build walls around the things we want to hide."

"What do you want to hide, Kendall?" he asked softly.

Ignoring the question, she continued calmly. "It's human nature. We want to guess everyone else's secrets without giving our own away."

"And if someone wants to see beneath the surface?"

Kendall shrugged. "We make them dig for it. You know—make them prove themselves worthy of our trust. Of all the animals on this earth, we're the most suspicious of a hand held out in friendship."

Hawke pushed his bowl away and gazed at her with an oddly sober gleam in his eyes. "Sounds like you learned that lesson the hard way," he commented quietly.

She stared at him, surprise in her eyes, realizing for the first time just how cynical she'd become. Obeying some nameless command in his smoky eyes, she said slowly, "I've seen too much to be innocent, Hawke. Whatever ideals I had . . . died long ago."

He stared at her for a long moment, then murmured, "I think I'd better find a pick and a shovel."

Suddenly angry with her own burst of self-revelation, Kendall snapped irritably, "Why?"

"To dig beneath the surface." He smiled slowly. "You're a fascinating lady, Kendall James. And I think

. . . if I dig deep enough . . . I just might find gold."

"What you might find," she warned coolly, "is a booby trap. I'm not a puzzle to be solved, Hawke."

"Aren't you? You act the sweet innocent, telling yourself that it's the easy way. And it's a good act, very convincing and probably very useful. But it isn't entirely an act, is it, honey? There is an innocent inside of you, hiding from the things she's seen."

"You're not a psychologist and I'm not a patient, so stop with the analyzing," she muttered, trying to ignore what he was saying.

"You're a romantic, an idealist," he went on as if she hadn't spoken. "But you hide that part of your nature—behind a wall that isn't a wall at all. You've got yourself convinced that it's an act, and that conviction keeps you from being hurt."

Kendall shot him a glare from beneath her lashes. "Now you're not even making sense," she retorted scornfully.

"Oh, yes, I am." His eyes got that hooded look she was beginning to recognize out of sheer self-defense. "A piece of the puzzle just fell into place. But it's still a long way from being solved. And, rest assured, Kendall, I intend to solve it."

"Is this in the nature of another warning?" she asked lightly, irritated that her heart had begun to beat like a jungle drum.

"Call it anything you like."

"I could just leave, you know."

"You could." The heavy lids lifted, revealing a cool challenge. "But that would be cowardly."

Knowing—*knowing*—that she was walking right

into his trap, Kendall snapped, "I'm a lot of things, Hawke, but a coward isn't one of them!" And felt strongly tempted to throw her soup bowl at him when she saw the satisfaction that flickered briefly in his eyes.

"Good," he said briskly. "Then we can forget about that angle, can't we? And get down to business."

"Business?" she murmured wryly. "That's one I haven't heard."

"Well, I would have called it romance, but I didn't want you to laugh at me." He grinned faintly. "Men are more romantic than women, you know. I read it somewhere."

"Fancy that." Kendall stared at him. "Most of the men I've known let romance go by the board."

"Really? Then knowing me will be an education."